Kat's Dog

The Bite-Sized Shifter Series

By

Rose Bak

Kat's Dog
© 2021 by Rose Bak

Table of Contents

About This Book

Clothing designer Kat Phillips nearly lost her life escaping her hometown. The tiger shifter did the unthinkable: leave the streak and their autocratic and old-fashioned ways. She's clawed her way to independence, and finally she's in a place where she feels safe and stable.

Until a wolf walks into her store and insists that they are fated mates.

For contractor Stuart Grey it's love at first sight, for both him and his wolf. Kat insists that she doesn't feel the same, but even the strongest tiger can't fight fate forever.

Cats and dogs might be enemies, but a tiger and a wolf just might be able to find their forever love...with a little luck. Stuart just needs to find a way to convince his reluctant mate that he's not a threat to her. And he's willing to enlist everyone in their small town to help.

"Kat's Dog" is book two in the "Bite-Sized Shifters", a series of paranormal romantic comedies you can read in just a few hours. Each book in the series is standalone featuring a mature couple, steamy scenes, a lot of fur and claws, and a guaranteed HEA.

Want a free book? Sign up for my newsletter[1] to be the first to know about new books and special sales. No spamming, I promise. Click here[2] to sign up for my newsletter and get your free book.

This book includes a special excerpt from "Until You Came Along", book one of the Oliver Boys Band series.

---

1. https://storyoriginapp.com/giveaways/62ee758e-068f-11eb-904e-c373f6014fe1

2. https://storyoriginapp.com/giveaways/62ee758e-068f-11eb-904e-c373f6014fe1

Dedication

For everyone who had to start over.

Kat

She felt the air still an instant before the hair on the back of her neck rose. *Danger,* something deep inside called out. Kat felt her claws start to lengthen and her muscles tighten as she stepped away from the rack of clothing she was organizing.

She turned around and almost fell over as her tiger began pawing crazily in the back of her mind. *He's here! Finally, he's here!*

Her tiger was gleeful, but Kat was confused. *Who?*

She looked around to see what was going on and then she saw him. A tall man striding towards her. Well, stalking towards her really, like she was prey, his gaze laser focused on her. Kat straightened her spine as the man stopped a few feet away from her, a look of shock and wonder on his face.

And what a face it was. The man was white, ruggedly handsome, with strong cheekbones and a square jaw lightly covered with scruff as if it had been a day or two since he had shaved. His hair was light brown with golden highlights that came from the sun rather than a fancy salon and his eyes were a pale green.

He was built like a damn mountain. His body was bulky but clearly all muscle.

Several inches over six feet, he towered over Kat's five foot eight frame. His shoulders were wide and straight over biceps that bulged against the confines of his short-sleeved shirt that matched his eyes. A trim waist led down to thickly muscled thighs, lovingly covered by faded denim. His brown work boots were battered, as if he had worn them for many years.

Shifter, she thought. *Wolf.* She didn't need to sniff him to tell, she could see the wolf in his eyes, looking out at her. The tiger inside her recognized a fellow predator immediately.

Their eyes met and held, and a sense of shocked recognition hit her. Meanwhile, her tiger yowled in joy.

Mate! Mine!

As if hearing the internal call, the man's eyes heated up and a smile split his handsome face. Kat felt certain her tiger was as visible to him as his wolf was to her.

"Mate!" he exclaimed, his voice every bit as joyous as her tiger's internal voice.

Kat stiffened as his words registered. In her mind she forced her tiger back into the corner, telling it sternly to lay down and be quiet. It was a struggle, but the tiger finally laid down with an annoyed whimper.

Damn it, she had hoped this moment would never happen. Had assumed it would not. She had heard the stories of course. "Fated mates" was the ultimate fairy tale for shifters. It was the stuff of story books – the idea that fate, the universe, the gods, whatever it was you believed in, had brought you the one person in all the world who was perfect for you, the other half of your soul.

What a load of crap.

Kat had learned young that being the mate of a male shifter meant being controlled. Put down. Treated like property.

The tiger streak she had grown up with in Montana was very traditional. The men went to work, and the women were like indentured servants. The women cleaned the house, cooked all the meals, took care of their cubs that came in rapid succession, and catered to every whim of the demanding males in their lives under the guise of matehood.

And the alpha, the leader of their streak, had absolute authority. He served a god-like role, telling people what work to do, who to mate, how to behave. Independence was not allowed. Failure to be subservient to the alpha or your mate earned you a smack across the face – or worse.

No thank you, Fate.

Kat had worked hard to escape her past. She had barely escaped the streak with her life when the streak's alpha wanted to marry her off to some asshole who served as one of his enforcers. A cruel tiger more than twenty years her senior. *Gross!*

Leaving her streak had been like leaving a gang – she was beaten nearly to death for her impudence. But she had survived, had built herself up out of nothing. Along the way she had promised herself that nothing, and no one, would ever control her again.

Now, years later, she was finally in a good place, with a great new job in a brand new town that she loved. There was no freaking way she was going to give that all up to be a maid and breeder for some asshole alpha wolf. Even if he was staring at her like she was the last cupcake in the bakery.

"Oh no!" Kat said loudly and emphatically. She narrowed her eyes and gave him her meanest glare. "No. No, no, no!"

The man crinkled his eyebrows in confusion. He really was quite attractive. If he didn't think they were mates she would love to scratch an itch with him. It had been a while since she had been with anyone.

"Mate, what's the m....," he started.

"I said no, and I mean no. Whatever you're thinking, I'm not interested. Now run along," she ordered in the same firm voice she used on the stray cat that hung out in the ally.

It was an actual cat, not a shifter cat, just to be clear. In this town it could be either.

"Go on now, get out of here."

She pointed at the door but instead of leaving he stepped closer, his masculine scent surrounding them. Kat willed herself to resist the instinct to step back, to turn tail and run away as fast as she could. He reached forward and touched her arm softly with one long finger.

Her breath caught in her throat and for a nanosecond everything inside her became quiet, even her tiger. Then she felt an electric jolt buzz between them, shocking some sense into her. She angrily pushed his hand away from her and took a step back.

"Are you deaf?" she asked harshly. "I told you to go away."

"But you're my mate," he said in confusion, his head cocked to the side like the canine he was. "I know you can feel it. We thought we would never find you."

Kat stepped closer again and jabbed his chest with her pointer finger. It was rock hard so there wasn't much to jab.

"Listen here buddy," she hissed angrily. "I don't want a mate. I don't want you. Now be a good dog and scram."

The stranger seemed to shake off his daze. He frowned at her and her inner tiger whined. *You're upsetting our mate.*

"You're mine, little kitty," the man growled, his chest puffing up. "Fate has brought us together."

"And fate can bring us right back apart," Kat said harshly. "I don't believe in fate and I don't believe in mates. Now go away. I mean it. Forget you ever met me, and don't talk to me ever again."

She turned on her heel and strode towards the back of the store, seeking the safety of the work room where she worked on her designs. It was all she could do not to run, but there was no way she wanted to show him how much he had affected her. She slammed the door and fell against it, sinking to the floor. Her breath came in short pants and she dropped her head in between her knees, staving off the dizziness and panic.

The instinctive desire to be with the man – *with our mate,* her tiger corrected her – was intense. She had to fight it. She had seen women lose themselves before and vowed that would never happen to her.

She had worked too hard and given up too much to escape the confines of her birth streak. She had worked hard to get her own life. Now that she had it, she wanted to keep her independence. She wanted her own interests. She wanted to be happy.

We can have our mate and still be happy, her tiger whined.

Kat ignored her and sent up a prayer to every deity in the heavens that her mate would get the message and leave her alone. She liked this town, and she liked this job. She really didn't want to have to move again.

Stuart

What the hell had just happened?

Stuart walked out of the store on leaden feet, ignoring the salesgirl at the front wishing him a nice day.

Nice day? How could have a nice day when he had finally found his mate, after thirty-seven long years, only to be rejected? He hadn't even gotten a chance to talk to her. She appeared to dislike him on sight for some reason.

I don't even know her name, he thought dejectedly.

This wasn't how it was supposed to go. Normally two shifters saw each other and once they recognized that they were fated mates, they were immediately in a relationship. He knew shifters who had felt the mate pull so strongly that they'd been having sex within ten minutes of meeting. But his mate didn't even want to be in the same room as him.

Without a conscious thought, he headed towards his parents' house. It was a short walk from main street where all the shops were. Where his mate was.

The town of Greysden was originally a wolf town. Settled by grey wolves, their community eventually filled with other types of shifters. Bears. Lions. Tigers. Jaguars. Even a few of the smaller shifters, like weasels and bunnies.

Although shifters had been "out" to the human population for a generation now, most humans remained in denial and many shifters still preferred to have their own communities. It was nice to be around people who understood the challenges of sharing a body and soul with a mystical animal. It was also nice to not have people look at you weird when you woke up naked in the park after a good nighttime run.

Stuart replayed the last few minutes as he ambled up the sidewalk, trying to figure out what had gone wrong. He had been walking back from having lunch with a friend when he passed the boutique clothing store his cousin Gina owned.

"Gina's Closet" sold something called "reclaimed fashion". He didn't know squat about fashion, but Gina had explained it involved taking clothes that were out of style or donated to thrift stores and turning them into something new and stylish. Gina had a stable of designers she worked with on consignment, and also created her own designs in the store.

He had heard from his mom that Gina's store was doing so well she had recently hired another designer as an employee to help create their unique designs. Apparently that was his mate.

As he had passed the store, Stuart's wolf had gone crazy, pushing against him so hard he had fought to not shift on the spot. When he opened the shop door he had smelled her. His mate. He had known, even before he had seen her face, that she was the one. The one person who was his soulmate. It sounded cliché but it was like being struck by lightening the minute he saw her.

You'll know when it happens, his father had told him about meeting his mate. *It's instantaneous.*

Dad was right. If he hadn't believed his nose, he would have known the minute their eyes met. Everything in him had stilled, and in an instant he had felt a connection to her that he knew instinctively could never be severed.

She had felt it too. He saw the flare of awareness in her huge brown eyes, quickly followed by fear. He had seen her cat pushing to get to him before she got it under control.

His mate was beautiful. She was white and appeared to be mid-30s, close to him in age. Average height for a woman, her body was softly curved with generous hips and breasts offset by a defined waist. Her long wavy hair was dark brown, almost black, and her skin was smooth and golden brown, as if she spent a lot of time outside. She was perfect.

When he touched the silky skin of her arm he had felt a jolt of connection that had almost knocked him on his ass. He had felt completely euphoric. At least until she told him to go away.

In all the times he had imagined meeting his mate, he never once considered that she would hate him on sight.

"She rejected me as soon as I opened my mouth," he grumbled to his parents fifteen minutes later. "Looked at me like I was something gross she had stepped in."

"Whatever did you say to her?" Mom asked curiously as she slid a cup of hot chocolate towards him. With marshmallows. It was the middle of summer and he was thirty-seven years old, but his mother firmly believed that hot chocolate with marshmallows made everything better.

He took a sip and he had to admit, it did feel comforting.

"I called her my mate," he answered. "And she kept saying 'no' over and over in a voice like I was a puppy eating her shoe. She told me doesn't believe in fate or mates. Then she told me – quite forcefully—to get away from her and stay away."

"Are you sure she's your mate, son?" Dad asked. He always played the devil's advocate when one of them had a problem.

Stuart lifted his eyebrows. "Dad, seriously? How was it when you met Mom?"

"I knew instantly she was my soulmate," his father replied. His hand found his mate's and he gave her a secret smile before turning back to Stuart. His parents were still as in love today as they had been when they met forty years ago. It was inspiring.

"Everything stopped inside me, and then I felt completely at peace for the first time in my life," Dad confirmed.

"Yeah, that's how I felt too," Stuart said glumly. "Until she poked me in the chest, said she didn't want me, and ran away."

"Is she a bunny or something?" Mom asked. "Was she scared of your predator?"

"No, she's a tiger I think. Definitely one of the big cats," he responded.

"Well that's weird." Mom stood up and patted his shoulder. "Why would any girl in her right mind reject you? Let me get you some cookies to go with your hot chocolate."

He was going to need more than comfort food to figure this out. But he wasn't foolish enough to say no to Mom's baking. He looked at his father's thoughtful face.

"Even though the mate sensation is instantaneous, sometimes one party is…skittish," Dad said. "It's rare, but there are some shifters who reject their fated mate. Maybe she's afraid, or she's had a bad experience. Or maybe she's one of those new thinking women who thinks fate is a bunch of bullshit."

"Now that you mention it, my friends Valerie and Colt had some challenges getting together," Stuart said thoughtfully. "She was totally against being mates, and Colt really had to work to get her to trust him. It took a lot for him to convince Valerie to give them a chance, although they're really happy now."

His best friend Colt had met his mate after he had fallen off a cliff in his wolf form and been taken to Valerie's veterinary clinic by a human who had mistaken him for a large dog. Despite both of them knowing that they were fated mates, Colt had initially had a lot of trouble convincing Val to give him a chance after she rejected him, but she had finally come around and accepted Colt.

"Sounds like you're going to have to have to take the same approach son, you have to….woo her," Dad said.

"It won't hurt you to work for it," Mom added mischievously. It was a running joke in their family the way women threw themselves at Stuart. He had done a fair share of dating, that was true, but he had never been serious about anyone before now. His wolf had no interest in investing too much time in a woman who wasn't their mate.

"Woo her?" he asked. "Like how?"

"You know. Flowers. Gifts. Or find some way to spend time with her, maybe as friends, until she can't resist you," Dad explained. "She'll have to give in eventually. If you're really fated mates, the mate bond is too strong to ignore for too long. Not without a lot of pain for both of you."

Mom leaned over and gave him a hug. "No one could spend time with you and not see what a great man you are," she said loyally.

"Spend time with her….," Stuart said thoughtfully as he squeezed his mother's shoulder. "I think I know just the thing."

Kat

"How's it going Kat?"

Kat looked up from her sewing machine to see her boss, Gina, smiling at her. Kat was working on re-tooling an 80s prom dress into a sophisticated cocktail dress. This job at Gina's Closet was a dream come true. She got to help create new fashion while learning about running a retail operation.

It was so much cooler than her previous jobs. Kat had escaped her birth streak when she was eighteen, soon after she had graduated from high school. She had moved quite a bit over the last eighteen years, trying her hand at everything from bartending to reception work to working in an Amazon fulfillment warehouse.

The one constant in her life had been her sewing and fashion design work. She had been making her own clothes since her curves came in at thirteen. With wide hips and a narrow waist and what a bully in high school once referred to as her "linebacker shoulders", it was impossible to find clothes that fit her properly. Her birth family hadn't had a lot of money for more than the necessities anyway.

In fact, a used sewing machine was the first thing she had purchased when she finally got a job and was able to move into her first craphole apartment. It was her most prized possession to this day.

She met her boss Gina at a thrift store about an hour from Greysden. They had both been eyeing the same skirt and struck up a conversation about how they each wanted to modify that dowdy piece into something that was actually wearable.

When Gina found out that Kat had created the outfit she was wearing out of thrift store finds, she had been impressed. When Kat showed her pictures of her other designs on her phone, Gina had offered her a job on the spot. She had even helped Kat find a clean but affordable apartment rental over the local veterinary clinic, less than a mile away from work.

Kat couldn't believe someone was actually paying her to do the same thing she had done as a hobby for years. And she was paid well too – a "per piece rate" as well as a sales commission as a bonus. For the first time in her life, she had a job she loved.

"It's going great Gina," Kat answered her boss. "I'm almost done taking out the seams here."

Gina nodded with approval. "Awesome. You know I'm going to be at that trade show this weekend."

"Yes, I remember," Kat said.

"I just wanted to give you a heads up that my cousin Stuart will be here. He's going to build me some more shelves in the storeroom this weekend," Gina told her. "You don't need to do anything – he's got a key and knows where everything is. I just didn't want you to be startled if you saw a strange guy hanging around."

Kat nodded. "Great, thanks for letting me know. And have fun at the trade show."

"Thanks, maybe my mate will be there." Gina gave her a wink.

Kat rolled her eyes at the boss who was becoming a good friend. "You don't really believe that fated mate stuff do you?" she asked curiously.

"I don't not believe it," Gina responded. "A girl's gotta have some hope. I'll see you next week. Don't work too hard."

The next day Kat was cutting fabric when she heard someone banging on the other side of the wall. *Must be Gina's cousin putting up the shelves in the storeroom,* she thought.

Her tiger was suddenly restless, pushing against her, urging her to get up. She took a sniff but wasn't able to smell anything different through the closed door of the work room. She couldn't think of anything that would rile up her tiger. It must just be restless.

"Be quiet you silly beast," she admonished as she mentally shoved the tiger into a cage. "I'm trying to work right now. I'll take you for a run later."

She tuned out the banging and continued to work until her stomach started to growl. Kat looked at the clock on her cell phone and started. She had been sitting here for a few hours now, totally engrossed in her work, and it was already past one o'clock.

No wonder you're hungry, she thought to herself as her stomach growled again. *You haven't eaten all day.*

Standing up, Kat stretched her back with a groan. She had been sitting too long. She grabbed her purse from her desk drawer and set it on the table, intending to go find some lunch after she visited the restroom.

She had scarcely stepped foot into the hallway when she heard the door to the storeroom across the hall open. She looked up, way up, and gasped, her heart racing. It was the wolf from yesterday. Had he been waiting for her?

Her tiger jumped around happily, shaking its tail. *It's him! Our mate!*

"Good afternoon," he said amiably. His eyes slowly traveled down the length of her body and back up to meet her gaze. His eyes burned with desire, and it was clear that he liked what he saw. His gaze felt like a physical touch, and she felt a shiver travel down her spine.

"How are you today, Mate?"

"Stop calling me that," she snapped, feeling immediately angry. "What are you doing here, wolf? I told you to leave me alone."

His wide smile told her he was pleased with himself. Why did he have to be so handsome when he smiled? She mentally shook herself instead of climbing him like a tree. Oddly enough, that suggestion came from her own mind, not her tiger.

For once we agree, her tiger purred.

"I'm here to work on the storage room," he said, his voice carefully neutral. "My cousin – who is your boss as I understand it – gave me a key and asked me to build her some shelves."

Of course, this guy knew Gina. It was just how her luck worked. She had no illusion that him being here was a coincidence. She scowled and started to move past him, but his bulky frame was blocking the narrow hallway.

"Move!" she growled, trying to tamp down her anxiety about being trapped in the hallway with him. She had always hated feeling trapped. Yeah, that was the reason that her pulse was racing and it felt like her lungs couldn't get a full breath. It had nothing to do with the handsome and compelling guy in front of her.

His smile widened. "Why the rush to get away, little kitty? Do I make you nervous?"

Before she could answer, her stomach growled again. Loudly. His expression immediately changed to concern. "You need food, mate."

"I have a name god damn it!" she snarled as she shoved him aside with all her strength. "Now get the hell out of my way."

He moved easily enough that she knew he had allowed her to do it. There was no way she could have moved him otherwise. She was tall for a woman, and her tiger made her strong. But the man was big and solid and also had shifter strength.

To her annoyance, he trailed her up the hallway and out the back door of the store. They paused in the alley behind the store, and she whipped around to glare at him.

"Can I buy you lunch?" he asked, a smirk tilting up the side of his mouth.

"No. Leave me alone."

Her tiger sliced at her with its claws, angry about the way she was treating their mate.

"Then how about dinner tonight?" he asked. "We should talk about what happens next."

Kat stopped and whirled to face him again, resisting the instinct to shove him against the brick wall, and wrap herself around him like a monkey on one of those nature channels.

Had he been this good looking yesterday? And he smelled delicious too, even though the light sheen of sweat on his skin told her that he had been working hard. He was just so...deliciously big and male. Her entire body tightened with arousal. Good lord. It was like he was the last sprig of catnip on Earth, and all she wanted to do what to roll around in his scent.

Be strong, she reminded herself. *This guy is dangerous.*

"Listen buddy...," she started.

"It's Stuart actually. Stuart Grey."

"Your name is Stuart?" she laughed despite herself. "Did your parents not like you or something?"

He grinned back, totally not offended. Never in a million years would she had pegged him as a Stuart. His nerdy name was completely at odds with how he looked, all tall and strong and yummy. And clearly a guy who worked with his hands, she thought with a tiny shiver.

He can work us with those hands, her tiger purred as they both eyed the hands in question.

"Stuart is a family name," he responded. "How about you tell me your name, since you don't like me calling you 'Mate'?"

She ground her teeth, eying her escape route down the alley. "It's Kat, actually. Kat Phillips."

Stuart chuckled. "Your parents named their daughter Kat? And you're a big cat? That's cute."

Kat ignored him, instead turning around, and moving away from him. She raced towards the street as if her tail was on fire.

"You shouldn't run from a predator sweetheart," he called after her. "You know it just makes us want to chase you more." His voice was deep with promise and she felt it in her bones.

Kat headed around the corner and away from Main Street, resisting the urge to look over her shoulder. Stuart didn't follow, but she could feel his eyes on her, watching. She swallowed a sense of panic.

She had been planning to work for a few more hours today, but now that that damn wolf was there – *our mate Stuart,* her tiger helpfully reminded her – she was just going to head home instead. It was Saturday anyway. She could do some more work later.

It wasn't until she got home she realized that she had forgotten her purse on her work table. Fortunately, it wasn't the first time that had happened, so she had a spare key hidden outside her place. Letting herself into her apartment on top of the vet clinic, she made a mental reminder to go back for her purse after dinner. By then she could be sure that Stuart was gone.

Stuart? Her alleged mate was a wolf named Stuart? He was already proving to be persistent. Just her luck. Damn alpha males, didn't know the word "no".

Kat rattled around the house for a few hours, doing laundry, scrubbing the tub, dusting the shelves, doing whatever she could do to distract herself from her encounter with Stuart earlier in the day. It wasn't like her to be this unsettled. She had long ago taught herself to compartmentalize her emotions, but something about Stuart made it hard to put him in a box and forget him.

To make her inner turmoil worse, the entire afternoon her tiger whined inside her, wanting her to go back and find Stuart and lick him and bite him and lift her tail for him.

Mate. We must mark our mate.

Little slut, she told her tiger. *Be quiet.*

By late afternoon she couldn't take the whining anymore. She decided to let her tiger out for a run. Maybe that's why she had been so annoying lately. She hadn't gotten enough exercise this week. Kat had been putting in long hours finishing up some designs for the upcoming summer festival events that Greysden had, and both she and her tiger were feeling restless and craving exercise.

"If you want to run, we need to stay in the woods," she told her tiger sternly. "We are not going to look for that wolf."

Her tiger sullenly agreed. Kat stepped out on her back porch and headed towards the trees. Her apartment over the veterinary clinic backed right up to the woods that separated this side of town from the base of the mountain. It was the perfect place for a shifter to have easy access to a place to run.

Of all the towns she had lived in over the years, Kat liked Greysden the best. She had never realized how much of a difference it would make to live in a town that was predominantly shifters. Sure, the humans knew of their existence, but they either ignored or feared their supernatural neighbors. Here in Greysden, she felt more normal.

Kat moved a few feet into the woods and quickly removed her clothes, stacking them beneath a bush. She took a deep breath and called forth her inner animal.

In the space of a minute Kat felt her bones snap and grow, her muscles lengthen and thicken, as fur sprouted out and her tiger took over their body. Claws extended as she dropped down to her four legs and fangs lengthened beneath her lips.

Her tiger was medium sized, orange with thick black stripes that matched the color of her hair when she was in her human form. The tiger snarled happily at being released after so many days trapped in her human body.

She took a minute to stretch, rounding her spine up and lengthening her front legs a few times. It felt good to be back in her tiger form, so connected with nature. She really needed to get out in this form more often. Exercise and fresh air kept both her and her tiger calm and happy.

Kat sniffed the air happily as she trotted deeper into the woods. In this form she could hear every sound more clearly and smell all the plants and animals in the vicinity.

Speaking of animals, let's find a snack, her tiger suggested as they took off through the trees at a fast pace. *We need to be strong for our mate.*

"Forget about that stupid wolf", she chastised the tiger. "Remember what we went through to escape being tied down to a mate?"

Her tiger chuffed in annoyance. *Our mate is not like those males in our birth streak,* the tiger argued. *Those males wanted to keep us down. Break us. Our mate will love us just as we are.*

"You're just feeling horny," Kat argued back. "You know nothing about this wolf. We just need to find a nice uncomplicated human to hook up with and then we will both feel better."

Her tiger snarled and increased its pace through the woods. Her paws ate up the ground as the tiger blazed a trail through the woods, running off its anger.

We'll see about that, human. There's no other male for us now. Just our mate.

Stuart

Kat didn't return to the store that day, not that Stuart was surprised. Based on her reaction to him, he had assumed she would continue to avoid him.

He spent the next couple of hours finishing up the shelves he had promised Gina. When he was done he prowled around Kat's work room, inhaling the scent of his mate, and looking for clues about what she was like when she wasn't running away. He could still smell her scent in the room hours after she left, a seductive blend of flower and spice.

He picked up the fabric she had been working on and wondered what she was making with it. Something wonderful he assumed. If his mate worked for Gina, he knew she was talented. When he spotted the purse that had been left behind on the work room table, he knew he had a great excuse to hunt her down. Maybe she would talk to him if he brought her purse to her.

Being mates should be good enough for her to be with us, his wolf said sullenly. His wolf had been moping around in his mind ever since Kat had run away from them earlier.

"Don't worry buddy, she'll come around," Stuart told him, hoping it was true. It had to be true. His chest already ached with the sensation of being away from his mate. He knew it would only get worse. Knowing that she would be feeling the same way gave him hope.

It was surprisingly easy to find someone when you lived in a small town. All he had to do was ask Kat's coworker at the store how to return the purse to her. The clerk had readily shared that his mate was renting out Valerie's old apartment over the veterinary clinic a short walk away.

The town vet had recently moved in with her mate Colt so it made sense that she would rent out her old apartment for some extra money. Greysden was mostly single-family houses, and apartments were at a premium. His mate had been lucky to find the place. He knew that

Valerie would have no trouble renting the apartment again after he convinced his mate to move in with him.

Today? His wolf asked hopefully.

He chuckled. Somehow he knew that it was going to take a little more effort than bringing a forgotten purse to convince his stubborn mate to quit fighting fate.

The veterinary clinic was one of the businesses outside of the main strip, set up against the woods that surrounded that side of town. The clinic took up the entire first floor. Kat's apartment was set up on the top floor of the clinic, accessible by a staircase at the back of the building facing the woods.

It was already nearing seven o'clock, so he took a chance that he could convince his mate to spend some time with him. He came prepared with a pizza in one hand and a six pack of assorted beers in the other. Stuart unselfconsciously wore her purse over his shoulder. It was pretty small, probably just enough to hold a wallet and her phone. He liked that his mate wasn't one of those women who carried those giant bags full of stuff.

As he neared the clinic he started to feel uncharacteristically nervous. Hopefully, she would let him in so they could talk and get to know each other over food. He scarcely knew her, yet he already had an intense desire to take care of her and provide for her.

Climbing the rickety stairs, he set down the pizza and beer on the porch and raised his hand to knock on her door. Before he made contact with the door his wolf jumped to its feet inside him, alerting him that she wasn't inside.

She's coming from the woods! Our mate is coming! That way!

Stuart picked the food back up and headed towards a picnic table on the far edge of the parking lot, just next to the woods. His instincts told him that's the direction she was coming from. He set the pizza, her purse, and the drinks on the picnic table, then turned to wait for his mate to arrive.

She emerged from the woods in her tiger form, gracefully stalking towards him, eyes snapping. Stuart growled deep in his throat. Kat's tiger pulled back her lips and snarled at him, the sound deep and menacing.

"Now sweetheart, don't be mad at me. I had to see you again."

She snarled again, stalking closer as he pointed at the table. "You forgot your purse at the shop. I figured you would need it. I also brought you pizza."

We must feed our mate, his wolf agreed.

He picked up the pizza box and shook it for emphasis, sending the delicious smell of cheese and sausage through the air.

The beautiful orange and black tiger stood near a tree about ten feet away from him, watching him carefully. Stuart wondered if she was going to turn tail and run. To his surprise, the air around her shimmered as the tiger suddenly turned into a woman. A very naked woman.

She scowled at him as he ogled her perfect body, desire hitting him in waves. His cock immediately jumped to attention, pressing against his zipper painfully, and it was all he could do not to race towards her and claim her. Their eyes met and held.

Kat shook herself, like she wanted to clear her head, and stepped back behind a bush. To his relief, she came back out again. To his disappointment, she had covered herself up with shorts and a tank top. She hadn't bothered with a bra, and he could see the hard points of her nipples poke through the thin fabric. His pants tightened even more as he resisted the impulse to lick his lips.

"What do you want Stuart?" she asked, her voice weary.

"You ran off so fast you forgot your purse at the store," he explained. "I thought you might need it tonight."

She raised one eyebrow, clearly calling bullshit. He decided to be honest.

"Please Kat, I just want the opportunity to get to know you a little bit."

She looked suspicious. "Why would we do that?"

"Because we're mates," he answered. "We should get to know each other."

It seemed obvious to him, but she clearly didn't agree. Her eyes narrowed to slits and he saw her chest move with a deep aggrieved sigh.

"I already told you I don't believe in that mate crap," she replied, annoyance in her tone. "And even if I did, I don't want a mate. Not now, not ever. I believe I've been excruciatingly clear on that point."

He nodded and walked slowly towards her, trying to make himself seem unthreatening, like she was a skittish horse. He reminded himself of his dad's advice to take his time and woo her.

"Well, maybe we can be friends then. You believe in friends right?"

Seeing her tiny nod, he continued. "Friends sometimes have dinner together. Besides, I did bring your purse to you. The least you can do is have pizza with me."

Stuart kind of hated himself right now, but he wasn't above a little manipulation if it helped him get closer to his mate.

She sighed again. "What kind of pizza did you bring?"

"Sausage."

"OK, but we eat outside," she said reluctantly as she looked longingly at the pizza box. "You can't come in."

"No problem." He would see her den some other time.

Kat went into the apartment and returned a few minutes later with paper plates, napkins, and a bottle opener for the beers.

He let out a sigh of relief that she had come back down. He was half convinced that she would go upstairs and not come back again. He held up the six pack. "I've got lager or IPA," he said. "I wasn't sure what you would like."

She looked a bit taken aback at his thoughtfulness. He wondered what that was about.

"I'll take an IPA," she told him with a small smile. "Thanks."

His mate settled into the bench across from him and served herself two slices of pizza before sliding the box over to him.

He took a few slices of his own, then looked up to find her watching him, her eyes unreadable. His wolf preened at her attention, wagging his tail inside Stuart's mind. Their eyes met and they stared at each other for a long moment before she turned away, visibly shaking herself. It felt like the temperature had increased twenty degrees.

He wondered what Kat knew about mates that made her so against them. While not every shifter found their fated mate, he knew that when you found that special someone both shifters felt an inexplicable pull towards each other. He certainly did.

The longer a shifter went without completing the mate bond, the worse it got. The legends said that a shifter could go feral if their mate rejected them or they were separated from their mate for too long. He believed it. He already felt a little crazy all day after she had fled from him in the store. His wolf had whined incessantly for him to find their mate.

Suddenly he remembered back when Valerie was rejecting his friend Colt. The poor guy had been a mess the longer his mate avoided him. Like Kat, Colt's made had been anti-mate. But at least they had worked it out in the end. Stuart hoped that he and his mate would have the same happy ending. Maybe he should ask the couple for advice. Maybe what worked for Colt would work for him.

Kat finally broke the long silence, pulling him out of his thoughts.

"So, what do you do Stuart?" she asked as she grabbed another slice of pizza. "Let me guess...you're an accountant?"

He smirked. "Do these look like the hands of an accountant?" he asked, raising his calloused palms in her direction. She shivered and he wondered if, like him, she was imagining him running his calloused hands over the silky softness of her skin. He hoped so.

"I own my own business," he told her proudly. "I'm a carpenter. That's why Gina asked me to build her shelves."

His mate nodded. Her dark brown hair slid over her shoulder and rested against her shirt. He followed it with his gaze. She was so beautiful. Kat cleared her throat, snapping his attention back to her face.

She picked up a slice of pizza and took a large bite, closing her eyes happily. "Mmm. This is good," she moaned.

Stuart started to sweat as his cock went from half hard to trying to punch through his jeans in about two seconds. Again.

"It's from Tony's. Best pizza in town," he responded. His voice sounded strangled to his own ears. It was hard to focus on their conversation while his wolf was begging him to pull Kat onto the table and fuck her into submission.

She nodded but didn't say anything more. He wondered if this intense curiosity about her was one sided. Somehow he didn't think it was. Yet she held herself back.

"So, tell me about yourself Kat," he asked, chewing his own pizza. "I know you're not from Greysden, but are you from Colorado originally?"

She shook her head. "No."

"Where did you grow up then?" he asked curiously.

"Montana," she answered shortly. Her expression was closed off, and she focused on her pizza instead of him.

"When did you leave there?" he prodded, watching her carefully.

"When I was eighteen."

"Where did you go then?" he persisted.

She sighed deeply like he was annoying her with his questions. "Here and there."

OK, so clearly his mate was not big on sharing. It would just make it that much sweeter when he broke through her defenses and had an honest conversation with her.

"I'm glad I saw your tiger, she is beautiful," he told her honestly.

She looked up at him, as if checking for a lie, then turned back to her food. "Thanks."

When she didn't add anything more, he added, "I'm a wolf. Grey wolf."

"I know." She sighed again as if he were dancing on her last nerve. His mate had sighing down to a science.

Stuart was usually pretty even tempered, but his mate was starting to annoy him with her stand-offish attitude and put-upon sighs. He dropped a half-eaten slice of pizza onto his plate and leaned forward, resting his arms on the picnic table, and stared at Kat until she raised her eyes to his. One dark eyebrow lifted in question.

"What are we going to do about this mate thing?" he asked.

Mark her! Mate her! Make her ours, his wolf suggested helpfully.

"Nothing," she answered firmly. She mimicked his posture, leaning forward to rest her arms on the table. His mate was no pushover, that was for sure. He could almost see her fortifying the walls around her, although when her dark eyes met his, saw the mixed emotions in them that she probably thought were better hidden.

"I have told you this twice now Stuart. We are not mates. I don't want a mate."

"We are mates," he answered stubbornly. "And we will be together, Kat. There's no sense in fighting it. You will be mine. And I will be yours."

Kat

"Oh, so what I want means nothing?" Kat asked hotly, pushing herself to standing. Her chest was heaving with anger and nerves. She crossed her arms and glared at the infuriating wolf. Did he think all he needed to do was bring pizza and beer and she would abandon her principles and fall at his paws?

Stuart stood up as well, extricating himself from the picnic table seat and stalking towards her. Before she could stop herself she took a step back. Stuart's eyes flared with excitement as he stalked closer.

Kat willed herself to be still. *Show no fear*, she reminded herself. He might be a predator, but so was she. She hadn't gotten this far in her life backing down from a fight. She had a quick memory of pain as she remembered the beating she took leaving the place where she had grown up.

There's nothing to fear from our mate, her tiger said indignantly.

Her tiger had no idea. The tiger thought in simple terms. Hunt. Eat. Run. Mate. But Kat knew better. This male was dangerous to them both. He had the power to take everything from them. She could tell from her strong reaction to him that she was in danger of giving in to him.

Stuart brought himself toe to toe with her. With only a few scant inches separating them she could feel the heat and aggression rolling off his big body. His distinctive scent wrapped around her and she fought her instinct to run. Instead, she met his gaze head on, refusing to back down. She'd be damned if she kowtowed to him, or anyone.

He stared deeply into her eyes, as if that would help him read her mind. And maybe it did because he asked, "Why does what's happening between us scare you so much, Mate?" he asked, his voice soft. "Finding your mate is supposed to be a cause for celebration. Who hurt you so badly?"

Kat puffed herself up and glared at him. "I am not scared," she lied.

He lifted one big hand and cupped her chin, his touch surprisingly gentle. "You're trembling, Mate."

"Stop calling me that!" she groused, shoving his hand away even as she longed to lean into the comfort of his body.

He studied her for a long moment. Her tiger was urging her to touch him, to move closer, and without conscious thought she felt herself sway slightly towards him as if he were tugging on an invisible string connecting them.

It was all the opening he needed. Within the space of a breath, he gripped her hips in his strong fingers and pulled them even closer together, lowering his mouth until it was a scant inch away from hers. She could smell the faint scent of pizza and beer on his breath.

"What are you doing?" she asked. She meant it to be forceful, but instead her words came out breathy and soft.

Instead of answering, he closed the distance between their lips, pressing against hers firmly. It felt like an electric shock and she gasped as every nerve in her body lit up at once. He took advantage of that gasp and slid his thick tongue in, boldly exploring the recesses of her mouth.

She stiffened at first, but then her mind shut down and she relaxed, leaning into the feelings. Surely it couldn't hurt to just have one kiss, right?

Sensing her acquiescence, Stuart pulled her closer, wrapping his arms around her waist and bringing his pelvis against the soft curve of her stomach. He was already hard as a rock and the woman inside her thrilled at his clear desire for her.

He tilted his head to change the angle and deepen their kiss. Goodness, Stuart was an incredible kisser. She had never had a kiss in her life that was this hot, this all-consuming.

Kat slid her arms up over his broad shoulders, playing with the hair at the nape of his neck as the kiss went on and on. She inhaled his masculine scent and leaned into his hard body as her tiger purred inside her.

Suddenly she felt lighter. He lifted her up to sit on the picnic table. Shoving her legs open wide, he moved to stand between them, pressing the hard length of his cock against her hot core. Kat moaned against his mouth and ground her pelvis against him wantonly, wondering if she could get off just with some kissing and dry humping.

Good lord, it had never felt this good before. She had been with a few men over the years, always full humans, and never for more than a few weeks. No one had ever made her body hum like this. It was like every kiss she'd ever had was just practice for this moment. Stuart's kiss was overwhelming. She dug her nails into his biceps and wrapped her legs around his hips, pulling him as close as possible.

Her body was vibrating with need and she realized that she was purring in the back of her throat. Her tiger hovered close to the surface, begging her to release her fangs so she could mark Stuart and tell the world he was taken.

Stuart finally broke the kiss and she gasped for breath. Sliding his lips down the side of her neck, he began leaving a trail of small bites along the delicate skin. When he reached the point where her neck met her shoulder he bit her a little more firmly, not breaking the skin but giving her enough pressure that that her body understood his intentions.

Our mate wants to mark us, her tiger said joyously. *Tell him yes.*

It was like someone had thrown a bucket of cold water over her. Kat lowered her hands and shoved against his chest as hard as she could. Taken off guard, Stuart stumbled back, his face adorably confused.

"What's the matter?"

"Keep your damn teeth to yourself, Wolf!" she yelled as she leapt off the picnic table and rushed around to the other side, needing a barrier between them. He had the nerve to look hurt, and that only increased her feelings of confusion. What was happening?

That kiss. Oh my god. It was incredible. It was life changing. It scared the hell out of her. If kissing Stuart could affect her so deeply, what would it be like if they had sex?

WHEN we make LOVE, her wolf corrected. *Not "if".*

Her breath was coming in short gasps as she tried to catch her breath. Her mind raced in a frenzied panic. She knew in that moment that this man had the power to ruin her, without a doubt. She couldn't let that happen.

She backed away from him, snatching her purse off the table and walking backwards towards the stairs that led to her apartment. She kept her eyes on him the entire time, waiting for him to pounce.

"Where are you going, Mate?" he asked, still seeming confused at her change of mood. Clearly all he thought had had to do was kiss her and she would fall into his arms and give him what he wanted, she thought cynically. He took a step towards her, then stopped again as she growled at him.

"I. Don't. Want. A mate!" she ground out, glaring at him. "Leave me alone, damn it."

"You know I can't do that Kat," he said softly. "My wolf won't let me stay away from you any more than your tiger will let you stay away from me."

He's right, her tiger agreed. *Our mate understands us.*

Kat ignored it. Her mind was racing.

"Look Stuart," she said, deciding to reason with him. "Clearly there's an attraction between us, I won't deny that. But I know that you have bought into the fated mate fairy tale, and that's not what I want. Not now, not ever. There's no sense starting anything between us when it's doomed to fail."

His face fell and she felt like a total jerk. She didn't want to hurt him, truly, but she had to protect herself.

"I have worked too hard in my life to be independent, to escape where I came from," she continued. "No matter what my tiger or your wolf wants, I am still in charge of my own destiny. You can't change my mind on this, no matter how incredible if feels when you kiss me."

"Kat. Mate." He reached out as if to move towards her again and she held up her hand, palm facing towards him in the universal "stop" signal.

"I appreciate you bringing my purse and bringing pizza Stuart, but this is goodbye. Please don't bother me again."

"But..."

"No. There's no 'but'. I don't want what you want, and I'm going to ask you – again – to leave me alone," she told him. "You should go find a nice wolf who will make you happy. I'm sure lots of girls would be thrilled to be your mate. But I'm not them. Even if I wanted a relationship, I'm too fucked up to be a good mate. Trust me on that."

He opened his mouth to respond and once again she gave him the "stop" signal.

"Goodbye Stuart, good luck finding what you're looking for."

She could feel his eyes on her as she forced herself to walk calmly up the steps of her apartment. She sighed with relief as she entered the safe space of her home. She turned around to see him still watching her from below. She ignored his devastated look the same way she ignored the hissing of her tiger and closed the door behind her. Kat had learned a long time ago that she needed to look out for herself, because no one else would. She wasn't going to stop now.

Our mate will look out for us! Her tiger was sullen and angry. Kat shushed her.

Suddenly exhausted, Kat headed right to her bedroom and fell face first onto her bed, fully clothed. She fell asleep immediately and had restless dreams about Stuart all night.

She woke up early Sunday morning, still wearing her clothes and laying on top of the comforter. Despite sleeping for so long, she still felt tired. Rising with a groan, she took a long hot shower to loosen up her sore muscles.

Yesterday she had run her tiger to near exhaustion, trying to get a certain grey wolf out of both of their heads. At least until he showed up at her place anyway. The run left her physically spent, and their conversation – and that crazy hot kiss – left her emotionally exhausted.

After pulling her damp hair into a braid, Kat examined the paltry contents of her fridge. It was slim pickings. And she was out of coffee. Damn.

"Time to go shopping," she told herself. "But first, breakfast."

Gathering a couple of reusable shopping bags, Kat headed towards the main commercial area of Greysden. She owned a car, but she hadn't driven it in weeks. Pretty much everything in Greysden was walkable, and she enjoyed being able to move her body as she went about her day.

Like every small town in America, Greysden had its own diner. It was run by a diminutive Greek couple in their 60s named Xenakis. They were both some kind of badger species that mostly were found on the island of Crete. How they wound up in Greysden, Kat had no idea. The food was hearty and delicious. She usually stopped in for breakfast on the weekends, and they always greeted her like a long-lost daughter.

"Ah, Catalina, welcome." Mr. Xenakis greeted her with a hug. After a lifetime of avoiding physical contact, Kat had been taken aback at how physically affectionate this couple was. After several weeks living in this town, she had grown used to it.

"Good morning Mr. Xenakis," she said, gently extricating herself from the hug. "I would love some breakfast."

"Of course Catalina, please sit anywhere."

Kat slid into a booth in the back, her stomach growling as the scent of bacon and coffee reached her nose. She was starving. She looked around the dated but spotless diner with a smile. She really liked it here in Greysden.

Mr. Xenakis had just returned with a menu and a cup of coffee for her when Kat felt the hair on her neck raise. Her tiger leapt up with excitement.

"Good morning, Mate." Stuart gave her a cheerful smile as he slid into the space across from her. The nerve of this wolf to make himself at home at her table. She gave him a sharp kick to the shin, but he just raised one eyebrow in amusement.

"Are you stalking me now?" she hissed, aware that gossip was the local pastime in Greysden. She had learned long ago that it was safer to stay under the radar wherever she was living. She hated drawing attention to herself.

Before Stuart could answer Mr. Xenakis was back, bringing Stuart his own menu and coffee.

"Good morning Stuart, you are friends with our Catalina?" the older man asked, clasping Stuart's shoulder in greeting.

"Yes, she's my mate," Stuart drawled, his eyes daring her to contradict him.

Mr. Xenakis clapped his hands together, a large happy smile splitting his face. "Oh my god, this is wonderful news," he exclaimed. "Catalina deserves a good mate and you two are perfect together. You will have a happy life, god willing, and have many beautiful babies."

Kat opened her mouth to respond, then closed it again, loathe to dim the older man's obvious enthusiasm.

"Nia!" Mr. Xenakis bellowed. His wife stuck her head through the window that separated the kitchen from the dining room, looking at him questioningly.

"Stuart has finally found his true mate," he continued loud enough to wake the dead. "It is our little Catalina! Such great news."

Every pair of eyes in the diner swung in their direction. Kat kicked Stuart again. "I'm going to kill you!" she whispered furiously as she felt her face flush with embarrassment.

He just shot her a cocky smile. "Shall we order breakfast Mate?"

Stuart

"Operation Woo Kat has begun," Stuart told his parents as he joined them for dinner later that night.

His sister Susan looked up curiously. The two siblings had been coming to Sunday dinner with the parents ever since they had left the den. Their mother insisted that they have family time once a week and truthfully they all enjoyed spending time together. Theirs was a close family.

"So it's true?" Susan asked. "You've met your mate?"

Stuart nodded.

"I heard it in the grocery store today," she told him, her tone mildly reproving. "Imagine hearing such big news from Myra the cashier instead of from your own brother!"

Stuart shot her an apologetic smile. "Sorry sis, it's all been kind of sudden. Things are kind of...complicated."

"Where is she?" Susan asked. "Is she joining us for dinner tonight?"

Start's smile dropped. "Not exactly." At his sister's curious look, he told her about his first meeting with Kat and his subsequent efforts to convince her that they were mates and should be together.

"She's adamant that she doesn't want a mate, even though I can tell she feels the pull as much as I do."

"Did you say she's from Montana?" Susan asked.

Stuart nodded.

"They have some weird ass shifter groups out there," Susan said. "Lots of survivalist types who cling to the old ways."

"What do you mean?" their mother asked.

"I have a friend who used to work in the Shifter Police out there," Susan explained. "His territory covered Montana, Idaho, and Wyoming. He said once you get outside the cities, some of those shifter groups are almost like cults. They hate outsiders and are totally cut off from the rest of civilization. The alpha rules with an iron fist, and the women are forced to be subservient. They have no rights and are considered to be property. They live in a culture of fear and intimidation. Maybe that's why she's against mating you."

Stuart flashed back to something Kat had said the day before.

I have worked too hard in my life to be independent, to escape where I came from. No matter what my tiger or your wolf wants, I'm still in charge of my own destiny.

Now he wondered if Susan was right and whatever happened to her in Montana had convinced her to avoid having a mate. He felt anger course through him at the idea that someone had hurt his mate.

Despite her annoyance with him, they had mostly had a nice breakfast earlier. At first all he could get out of her was one-word answers, but eventually he had drawn her into conversation. They had several common interests, and the conversation had started to flow between them. He was pleased to learn that much like him, his mate was smart and well-read, with general knowledge on a variety of topics.

They had both ordered a platter of breakfast foods, stacked high with eggs, bacon, hash browns, and French toast. By the time they were finished, there wasn't a crumb left.

After a minor skirmish over the check, he had paid for their breakfast under the proud watch of Mr. Xenakis. At least he and his wife were excited about Kat finding her mate.

Stuart had followed her to the grocery store and while Kat had mostly ignored him, she did allow him to carry her groceries home when it was obvious he was coming whether she wanted him to or not. Her back had gotten stiffer and stiffer as they had neared her apartment, the anxiety and irritation rolling off her so strongly that he didn't have to be shifter to pick up on it.

When they'd reached her apartment, Stuart had handed over her grocery bags without an argument, pressed a quick kiss to her forehead, and whispered, "I'll see you later, Mate."

She had still been staring after him in confusion as he'd turned the corner of her building, and Stuart had felt a perverse sense of satisfaction that he had thrown her off balance a little. He had been totally off balance since the day he'd met Kat.

"So, what's the next step in your plan, son?" his father asked.

"Remember when we had that stray cat that hung out in the yard?" he asked his family. "It just hung around all the time, joining us when we were outside, acting like he belonged here?"

Everyone nodded.

"After a while it was like the cat had always been there. We were feeding it and snuggling with it and letting it in the house and we were all totally attached to it? Well, that's my plan with Kat."

Susan snorted. "Your plan is to hang around until she gets used to you? Like some kind of persistent rash? That's so romantic."

"Do you have a better plan?" he asked his sister.

"You bet I do," Susan answered. "Remember how Colt got Valerie to talk to him?"

Kat

"You have a delivery."

Kat looked up from her sewing machine in confusion. Gina stood in the doorway holding a giant vase of assorted wildflowers. The arrangement was a riot of color, exactly the kind of arrangement Kat loved best. She had never been one for boring old roses. Not that anyone had ever sent her flowers before.

"Who's it from?" she asked her boss.

"Your mate!" Gina's voice was 100% "gotcha" as she walked over and placed the flowers on the corner of Kat's work table.

Kat rolled her chair back away from the flowers as if they would bite her.

"Ah, no, no no no, I don't want those!" She swung her head rapidly from side to side to emphasize her point.

Gina plopped down at the next table, watching Kat curiously. "Yeah I heard you were a bit skittish about the mate thing, but my cousin is a great guy. You couldn't ask for a better mate."

"That's the thing," Kat explained. "I didn't ask for a mate. I don't want a mate."

Gina took in her crossed arms and grumpy face and sighed. "Someday you're going to be mad at yourself for fighting this, Kat."

"I highly doubt that."

Yes you will, her tiger contributed.

Gina nodded. "OK well, I'll let you get back to work. Stuart said be sure to read the card."

Kat tried to go back to work but her eyes kept being drawn back to the flowers. It was...sweet. She fingered the card, almost afraid to read it.

Our mate is very considerate, her tiger offered.

With a sigh she pulled the card out from between the blooms.

"Beautiful flowers for a beautiful mate. Can I buy you dinner? Call me please."

The card was signed "S" with a phone number written underneath it. Kat crumpled the card in her hand, ready to throw it out, then at the last minute she smoothed it out and slipped it into her drawer. No sense wasting the flowers, even if she had no intention of calling Stuart. He would get tired eventually, right?

By Friday Kat was getting annoyed. She had five flower arrangements scattered around the room. One was delivered every morning this week. A second delivery came every afternoon, with her favorite drink – a coconut milk chai tea – and a cookie or muffin. Both were her usual orders from the bakery up the street, no doubt suggested by the bakery staff.

Clearly Gina wasn't the only one trying to sell her on Stuart. Not only had her boss had brought Stuart up every day, talking him up, sharing what a great guy he was, so had everyone else in town that she talked to. It was getting annoying.

It was just after 5:00 on Friday when Gina once again came into her workroom. "Hey, a few of us girls are going out to Murphy's for happy hour. You should come!"

Kat automatically shook her head. She had never been much for hanging out with groups of women. Gina looked hurt.

"I thought since you were new in town you could meet some of my friends," Gina said. "You can't just work all the time Kat, you need some balance too."

Gina looked so earnest that Kat relented. Gina was right, it would be good for her to make some friends. She was spending way too much time alone, either here at work or at home, and she had inexplicably been feeling a bit lonely.

"You're right Gina," Kat relented. "I'll come if you promise to not bug me about Stuart."

A weird look passed her face that Kat couldn't interpret, but Gina draw a cross mark over her heart with her finger. "I promise I won't say a thing to you about Stuart."

Three hours later Kat had to admit she was having a good time. In addition to Gina, their little group included a woman named Susan, and Kat's landlord Valerie. They were all wolf shifters except for Kat.

Their little group had commandeered a high top in the corner and were working on their third giant pitcher of margaritas. Shifters had a higher metabolism than full humans, but even as shifters they all had a nice buzz going on. Kat felt more relaxed than she had in years.

These were all strong, smart women who had brought her into their group with kind enthusiasm. She already felt like they had known each other for years. She had never laughed so much in her life.

True to her word, Gina had not brought up the topic of Stuart, for which she was grateful.

Val drained the last of her margarita and sighed. "I guess I should be going soon girls, I need to be at the clinic early for surgery." She picked up her phone. "I'm going to text Colt to pick me up. I told him I would let him know when I ready to go."

"Where is your mate tonight?" Susan asked. "Home?"

"No," Val responded. "He went out some place with Stuart."

Kat stiffened, and Susan's astute eyes immediately picked up on it. "Do you know Stuart, Kat?" Susan asked with what felt like forced casualness. There was some tone in the other woman's voice that Kat couldn't identify. It sounded almost – possessive.

"Yes," Kat answered shortly.

"I love him. He's really a great guy!" Susan said enthusiastically.

Threat! She wants to steal our mate! Her tiger shrieked in Kat's head, full of outrage.

"Are you guys, um, friends?" Kat asked cautiously, studying the other woman carefully. Her nails dug into her palms.

"More than friends," Susan laughed. "We've known each a long time. We're very...close."

Before she could register what she was doing, Kat leaned forward, staring at Susan aggressively. Her deep warning growl turned several heads in their direction.

Kat expected Susan to return her aggression, but instead she leaned back in her chair and started cracking up. "Oh my god, is the big kitty going to eat me if I get too close to Stuart?" she laughed, wiping a tear from the corner of her eye.

Kat growled again and continued to glare at Susan, aware that the other women were watching them avidly. It was taking all of her control to keep herself from shifting. Her tiger hovered just beneath the surface, ready to tear out the throat of the female who dared be so familiar with her mate.

"Susan, quit fucking with her," Gina chided. She put a calming hand on Kat's arm. "Susan is Stuart's sister, Kat."

Kat felt all the adrenaline leave her system as Susan continued laughing. "Stuart told me you weren't that interested in him, but I can see from that little display of jealous aggression that he's wrong."

Kat felt her face flush with embarrassment. She had never been jealous for even a moment before. Not once in her life. And yet, when she thought Susan's closeness with her mate was romantic, she was ready to fight for him. She wanted to gut the pretty wolf for being near her mate. What was wrong with her?

We will always fight for our mate, her tiger confirmed.

Val leaned forward and gave Kat a kind smile. "Kat, I was where you are right now a few months ago. Colt was all like, let's get mated, it's fate, yada yada, and I was resistant," she explained. "He kept coming around, bringing me gifts, being charming. I never wanted a mate, and I thought he was going to be some controlling jerk, but as I got to know him, I realized that fate was right, and he was the perfect guy for me."

Kat opened her mouth to argue, but Val held up a hand. "I'm just saying, take your time to get to know him. Move at a pace that works for you but be open to the possibility that there are forces at work that know what you need better than you do."

Kat slumped into her chair, completely flummoxed by the confusing array of emotions flooding through her. The other women kindly gave her some space, turning the conversation to other topics.

A few minutes later Val looked up with a smile as a tall, lean white guy came up to her. "Ah Colt, there you are. Are you ready to take me home?"

"Whatever you want baby," the guy said. He reached out and took Val's hand, pulling her to standing. The looked into each other's eyes and Kat was struck by how obviously in love they were. She had never seen two people look so happy before.

If only...her thoughts stuttered as she heard someone come up behind her. She recognized the scent before he spoke.

"Hi Mate! Having fun with the girls?"

Stuart

Stuart knew he owed his cousin Gina something nice for engineering this meeting with his mate. He had hoped that she would call him when he sent her the gifts, but although he had his eyes glued to his phone like a teenage girl, Kat never called him.

"We can kill two birds with one stone," Gina had told him. "The girls and I want to get to know her a little better, and then you can swoop in when we're done and see if you can get her to talk to you. Just act casual."

He dropped his bulky frame into the chair that Val had vacated, right next to his mate. His sister Susan was looking at him with her "I know a secret" eyes. He raised his eyebrows, but she shook her head slightly, communicating that she would tell him later.

She and Gina stood up, smiling at them both indulgently. "Well, we're going to get home too," Gina announced. "But you two should definitely stay and talk."

Kat leapt out of her chair like someone had electrified it. "I've got to go too. Thanks for inviting me Gina."

His cousin gave Kat a big hug.

"It was great to finally meet you Kat," his sister said, giving Kat a little wave. "Sorry about before."

Kat acknowledged the apology with a nod but didn't respond. As the other two women turned to go, Stuart faced his mate.

"Buy you another drink?" he asked.

She shook her head. "No. Thank you," she said formally, as if he were a total stranger. "I really need to get home too."

"I'll walk with you." She opened her mouth like she was going to argue, but clearly thought better of it.

"Whatever."

She set off at a brisk pace towards her apartment and he fell into step beside her, keeping silent. They had walked for about five minutes when she spoke up.

"Thank you for the gifts," she said, her voice grudging. "But I want you to stop sending me stuff."

"No."

She stopped on the sidewalk, spinning around to face him. "No?" she asked incredulously.

"That's right." Stuart resumed walking and she followed him, her face an adorable mixture of confusion and irritation.

"It's not going to help your case to ignore my wishes."

"According to you I don't have a case," he said mildly. "So why would that matter to me? Besides, whether you want to acknowledge it or not, you're my mate. I like providing for you. It makes my wolf happy."

Kat huffed with irritation but did not respond. She was silent the rest of the way back to her apartment, but he could feel her anxiety ratcheting up as they reached the vet clinic and walked around the back, just like when he had walked her home from the store last weekend.

Stuart knew she was wondering if he was going to try to make a move on her this time. He also knew she was conflicted. He could scent the smell of her arousal as clearly as the smell of her anxiety. The more time they spent together, the more he could tune into her emotions. That would only increase once they were officially mated.

She reached the stairs and turned around on the first step. The position brought her closer to his height. He stepped forward until only a couple of inches separated them. Awareness hummed between them as their eyes met and held in the dim light of streetlights.

"Look Stuart...," she started, her gaze dropping to his lips.

Stuart leaned forward and placed a chaste kiss on her cheek. "Goodnight Mate. Be sure to lock up."

He stepped back and watched her as she just stood there looking confused for a long moment. It was killing him not to grab her and kiss her until she softened against him like she had on the picnic table, but Susan was right. He needed to make her comfortable first. Get her to trust him.

With a final frown at him she climbed the stairs and opened her door, looking over her shoulder towards where he was watching her. "Well, goodnight then," she called, her voice sounding adorably confused.

He nodded and without another word, walked away. His wolf was screaming at him. *Mate! Don't leave her alone. Claim her!*

"We're playing a long game here wolf," he told his animal side. "Always leave them wanting more." He knew that he was starting to wear her down and with a little more time, Stuart hoped he could get her to accept him as her mate.

The next morning Stuart was fixing a faucet at his sister's house when the call came.

"Stuart? This is Mr. Xenakis. I thought you would like to know your mate just got here."

Stuart smiled. Apparently the whole town was getting involved in "Operation Woo Kat". Awesome. Word had gotten around fast about his mate's hesitation to give in to fate, and shifters were nothing if not romantic. Stuart appreciated it, knowing he could use all the help he could get.

"Thanks Mr. Xenakis, I'll be right there."

Leaving his tools on the floor, Stuart shot out of Susan's place and jogged the half mile to the diner. His mate was sitting in the far booth again, staring into space while she waited for her food to come. Her eyes widened as she saw him come up and slide into the booth across from her.

"Again?" she asked with an arched brow.

There was no heat there today. Instead, he sensed a bit of hurt and confusion about her, and he knew instinctively that keeping his distance last night had been the right thing to do.

"It's funny how we keep running into each other," he said innocently. "It's like it's meant to be."

Behind her head, Mr. Xenakis winked at him. Kat sighed deeply.

Just like the previous week, the two of them ate giant plates of breakfast food. He loved that his mate ate freely in front of him; he hated it when women nibbled on their food in front of guys.

Kat was back to offering only short answers when he tried to strike up a conversation, but he didn't mind. He knew instinctively that he was wearing her down. She was much more relaxed with him than she had been last week at breakfast, and she had only sighed at him once.

If Kat noticed that almost everyone in the diner was watching them, she didn't let on. When their meals were finished she snatched up the check before he could get it and marched up to the register to pay for both of their breakfasts.

"My turn," she called over her shoulder.

"Going shopping?" he asked as he joined her at the register. She was carrying reusable shopping bags, so it didn't take a lot of deductive skills.

"Yep."

"Mind if I tag along?" he asked.

"OK." He resisted the urge to give a little fist bump. She didn't sound particularly enthused, but at least that wasn't a no.

Stuart walked alongside Kat as she walked up the street, close enough that their shoulders were bumping occasionally. It was busy on Main Street and he called out greetings to several people he knew as they passed by. He noticed several people smiling when they saw him with Kat, but they wisely didn't say anything.

They entered the market, Stuart grabbing a basket for her and carrying it as he trailed behind her. Kat shopped quickly and efficiently, without a lot of dithering over which items to get.

They had just turned into the produce aisle when he heard a familiar voice call his name excitedly. "Stuart, sweetie!"

His mom was standing by the bin of oranges, her gaze moving curiously between him and Kat. Stuart wondered if this was a coincidence or if someone in town had alerted Mom that they were on their way to the grocery store. He wouldn't put it past his mother to engineer a meeting so she could scope out his mate.

Mom moved forward towards them with a huge smile. "You must be Kat."

Kat looked at her in surprise as his mother moved in to give her a big hug. She stood stiffly as his mom gave her a squeeze, then extricated herself. He wondered if she noticed that she had moved closer to Stuart, as if he could protect her from the strange woman hugging her in the produce aisle.

"I'm Gail, Stuart's mom," she told his mate. "I've been dying to meet you." Mom's eyes eagerly took in everything about Kat. Not real subtle, that one. She was probably measuring his mate for a wedding dress in her mind.

Kat looked panicked. "Um, I don't know what you heard Mrs..."

"Call me Gail, dear."

"OK then," his mate acknowledged. "I don't know what you heard Gail, but..."

His mother interrupted again. "Well Gina has told me all about your design talents. She showed me several of your clothing designs and I was blown away."

"Oh. Well, thanks." Stuart could practically hear her wondering if Mom knew they were mates.

"I'd love to get to know you better, Kat. You should come to our house for dinner tomorrow. We have a family dinner every Sunday night at six o'clock. I'll expect to see you there." Mom's voice was friendly but the order there was clear.

The panicked look returned. "Oh, that's very nice of you, Gail, but I, um, I have other plans."

"What plans?" Stuart asked. She shot him an annoyed look as he called her out on her obvious lie.

"Nonsense. We will see you tomorrow at six. Stuart will bring you over with him so you can find us," his mom continued.

Kat opened her mouth again, and Mom shook her head and shot Kat a stern look. "I absolutely insist you come, Kat. I won't take no for an answer."

"Clearly that trait runs in the family," Kat muttered under her breath. She narrowed her eyes and glared at Stuart like it was his fault that she had been backed into the invitation. Not that Stuart was unhappy about this turn of events.

Mom ignored his mate's obvious lack of enthusiasm and continued chattering on.

"You're not a vegetarian are you? Oh, what am I saying, of course you're not a vegetarian. Tiger. Duh."

She leaned over and kissed Stuart on the cheek before rushing away. "I'm looking forward to getting to know my new daughter," she called over her shoulder. "See you both tomorrow."

His mother was gone as quickly as she appeared. Kat looked a little shell shocked as she stared down the aisle where his mother had disappeared.

Stuart took her elbow. "Come on Mate, let's finish up your shopping so I can get you home."

She reached over and smacked him hard in the stomach with her tiny fist. "Thanks a lot!"

Kat

Stuart walked her home from the grocery store, staying one step behind her like some kind of silent bodyguard while she stomped along. She knew she was being a total bitch ignoring him, but she was annoyed that he had told his mother they were mates. Gail had manipulated her so skillfully she was almost impressed. She hated feeling like she had to go to their dinner or look rude.

She didn't want to look too closely at her reluctance to alienate Stuart's family. Normally she didn't worry too much about hurting people's feelings, but as much as she had wanted to argue with Gail and continue to refuse her invitation, she didn't have it in her. It was politeness, that's all, not any fear that she would start off on the wrong foot with her new family. Right?

Stuart wisely stayed silent as she fumed. When they reached her apartment, he handed over her groceries and left with a promise to pick her up for dinner the next day.

Kat stripped down as soon as she got home and headed into the woods. She ran her tiger until they were both panting with exhaustion. She stopped for a while near a stream deep in the woods, staring in the water in her tiger form with her head resting on her paws. Stuart seemed to be worming his way into her life whether she liked it not. What was she going to do about him?

Mate him! Mark him! Make him ours!

Ignoring her tiger side, Kat forced herself to get up and head home. Her tiger was moving much more slowly this time, and it gave her even more time to think about her situation. She liked her job. She liked living in Greysden. She even liked her tiny apartment. And, if she was being totally honest with herself, she liked Stuart too. And that scared the crap out of her.

Her mind wandered to the day she left her streak. She had been planning her departure for months, debating how to make her exit as easily as possible. The streak was like a cult or a gang – they did not tolerate deserters. Kat debated just running away, but the alpha would have undoubtedly sent the enforcers after her. If they had caught her, she would been imprisoned, or even killed. It had happened before.

In the end she requested a meeting with her parents and the alpha and laid out her case. She told them she wanted to leave. That she knew there was more for her out in the wider world, and she had no interest in mating the tiger that the alpha had designated for her.

The guy was one of his trusted men, at least twenty years older than her, and as mean as a snake. Her parents and the alpha had been pushing her to be with her appointed mate, and now that she was eighteen it was only a matter of time before he marked her, whether she liked it or not. Kat would rather die than be with him and in the end, she almost did.

The alpha had proclaimed that if she wanted to leave she would need to depart immediately. But there was a price.

"You came to this streak with nothing, and you will leave with nothing," he ordered imperiously. "Not even the clothes on your back."

What the alpha didn't know was that she had expected this. She had spent months spiriting away supplies and hiding them in a cave deep in the forest. The cave was about twenty miles away from streak territory, in a neutral zone that belonged to no shifter groups.

"You know what the price is for your departure Kathleen," he continued, lifting his hand to call over his beta. "Call the enforcers."

Kat had stared at the ground, forcing herself to show no reaction. The alpha expected her to grovel and beg and cow before his anger, but she refused to give him the satisfaction. Either they would kill her, or she would be allowed to leave under the ancient laws they followed. Either way she would be free.

They had all trudged to a clearing behind the main building where the alpha lived, and Kat fought against her fear. People she thought were friends, her family, and her neighbors gathered around to watch as Kat went through the requisite fifteen minutes of beating by the enforcers. The air was festive, as if they were about to watch a sporting event instead of several grown men attacking a young girl.

The alpha called for the beating to start, and the enforcers surrounded her, growling in threat and anger at her impudence for wanting to leave. It was rare for someone to voluntarily leave the streak, and even rarer for that person to survive the attack from the enforcers. Only the strongest survived. Clearly no one thought she had a chance.

Any hope she'd had that they would take it easy on a young girl was soon gone as five grown men tore off her clothes and started to beat her to a bloody pulp. The man who was supposed to be her mate was the most vicious. Her desire to leave was a particular insult to his male pride. Kat lay on the ground, curled up and trying to protect herself from the worst of the blows.

Sometimes late at night Kat could still feel their sharp kicks, the punches to the head, and the slices of the claws they extended even though they were to retain their human form. She could feel the searing pain in her body, smell the sick scent of her blood pouring into the ground. But what haunted her the most was the hurtful chants of the streak members as they watched with undisguised glee as she was beaten. "Slut. Slut. Slut." "Kick her! Kick her!"

Even her own parents joined in the taunting. They had made their choice, and it wasn't Kat. Not that she had been surprised. Her parents had always been offended by what they considered her being "uppity". They couldn't understand why she wanted more than this insular dysfunctional streak filled with violence and pain.

When the timer sounded the attack stopped the alpha called "time!" and all the enforcers backed up to give her some space. Aggression and anger and testosterone filled the air. She lay on the ground bleeding and shaking, her breath coming in shallow painful wheezes, all that her broken ribs would allow. She was totally naked, and not an inch of skin was left untouched by their violent attack.

Kat looked up at the leering faces around her and saw a glimmer of respect in their eyes that she had survived, that she had never begged for them to stop. Kat had seen grown men break under similar attacks. She knew then that after surviving the attack, she could survive anything.

"You are dead to us," the alpha had announced. "Get out. Now."

Unable to walk, she had crawled out into the forest on her hands and knees. Her progress was slow, and she almost passed out from pain several times, but she didn't stop until she had crossed the boundary into neutral territory. Until she knew she would be safe.

Kat spent two nights huddled in a hollowed-out tree as her body tried to heal itself. Even with her shifter healing, it was slow going. She was covered in bruises and long, deep scratches, with multiple broken bones. When she was strong enough to walk she made her way to the cave, relieved that no one had discovered her stash of clothing, food, and money.

It was another week before she was strong enough to shift. After two weeks living in the cave she finally was recovered, although some of the scars from her beating remained. Shifters didn't usually get scars, unless the wounds were deep enough to resist the healing process.

Kat considered her scars badges of honor. They had tried to break her, and they had failed. When she finally walked out of the cave, Kathleen was Kat. She was a new woman, strong and independent. She was a survivor. And no one could take that away from her.

As the years passed, the memory of that fateful day dulled, but she would never forget it. That's why meeting Stuart had thrown her for such a loop. He made her question her long-held conviction that she was better off alone.

Kat had been clear that she wasn't going to marry the cruel older man her alpha had selected for her, but with Stuart nothing was clear. She felt drawn to him in a way she never had been with anyone in her life. She dreamt about him every night, her unconscious sending her visions of them being together, getting married, her swollen with his pups. She just didn't know what she was going to do about this mate thing.

"Not a word from you," she said sternly, before her hussy tiger was able to make any more racy suggestions about what she should do.

Stuart knocked on her door right at 5:45 the next day. He looked incredibly handsome in khakis and a blue button-down shirt. His hair was a bit damp, as if he had just showered. She took a subtle sniff and caught a whiff of soap and shaving cream along with his usual heady scent.

He gave her a smile as his eyes moved from her head down to her feet, then back up again. When his eyes met hers they were burning bright with approval and arousal. Kat ignored the answering thrill of arousal that moved through her.

Unsure how to dress for a family dinner, she had chosen to wear a cute, flowered sundress that she had made out of a 1970s maxi skirt that she had picked up at an estate sale. She had tailored the red flowered fabric to hug her curves perfectly, with the hem falling just beneath her knees.

She paired the dress with a light green sweater that matched the leaves in the flower pattern on her dress, and a pair of brown cowboy boots. After more dithering than she would ever admit, she had left her hair down, falling straight to her shoulders in a dark curtain, and added a bit of mascara and shiny lip gloss.

"You look fantastic, Mate." Stuart's voice was deep and warm.

Kat rolled her eyes even as a flush of pleasure moved through her. "Thanks. Let's get this over with."

"Well, that's the kind of enthusiasm I love to see," Stuart said wryly.

She smirked at him as he led her to his battered navy pick-up truck. He bucked her into the passenger seat, and they made the short drive to his parents' house in silence.

"This is the place," Stuart announced as he pulled into the driveway of a cute Victorian house with yellow shudders and a large porch. The yard was well tended and filled with flowers and plants in neat rows. It looked comfortable and welcoming. It looked like somebody's home.

"Is this where you grew up?" she asked, curious despite herself.

"Yep. I lived here until I was twenty-one. Shall we?"

She suddenly felt nervous, which was totally unlike her. She never got nervous, not really. Until today. Meeting Stuart's family felt big, despite her protestations that they would not be together, and she didn't really know how to do a family dinner. Kat had never allowed herself to get close enough to anyone she'd dated to meet their family.

Growing up, most of their meals were in a group setting. Members of the streak sat at long communal tables, separated by gender. The females did all the cooking and cleaning, of course, while the males sat around talking and drinking. The dining hall was always filled with a lot of male aggression and posturing and female submission. Just thinking about that gave her a stomachache.

"You OK?" Stuart asked, studying her carefully. It was a bit creepy how easily he seemed to tune into her emotions already, no matter how hard she tried to conceal them. She knew that mate bond was getting stronger between them.

She nodded as she mentally shook herself. "Of course. Why wouldn't I be OK with having dinner with a bunch of strangers who think I'm your mate?"

He grabbed her hand, giving it a squeeze as they walked towards the house. "Promise me one thing. Whatever happens tonight, just tell yourself I was adopted."

She looked at him curiously. "You were adopted?" Adoption was rare in the shifter community.

"No," he laughed. "But sometimes when my family is driving me crazy, it makes me feel better to pretend that I was."

Stuart

He wasn't sure what he had expected when his mom had invited Kat for dinner, but it wasn't that Kat and his mom would immediately become best friends.

His mate hadn't been in the house for ten minutes before the two women were drinking and laughing as they worked together to make a big salad. His father was making chili in a huge pot on the stove, and his sister was slicing up Mom's freshly baked cornbread. That left Stuart to set the table.

Growing up it had always been like this – their whole family working together to prepare their Sunday dinners. During the week it wasn't unusual for one or more of them to be gone for extracurricular activities or because they had to work, but their parents had always been adamant that Sundays were family time. No exceptions.

"And then Stuart came running out naked from the waist down, like he was Donald Duck or something, tugging on his penis and joyfully showing us how he was making it longer!"

Kat was laughing hysterically at Mom's stories about Stuart as a tiny pup. He knew his mom well enough to realize that she was trying to endear him to Kat.

He studied her from beneath his lashes. Her smile lit up her whole face, making her even more beautiful. She looked up at him and their eyes met and held. Her smile faded as they stared at each other for a long moment until Susan called to them from the dining room, breaking the spell. "Let's eat!"

They sat around the same scarred wood dining room table where they'd been having family dinner for as long as he could remember. As always, Mom and Dad sat at either end, with Susan on one side and Stuart on the other. This time, he had his mate sitting next to him. He felt a rush of contentment. He loved having her at his side.

Kat had really loosened up here with his family, and he was grateful for the change in her. Happy to see her letting down her guard, if only for a while. Until his sister opened her big mouth.

"Do you get back to Montana to see your family very often, Kat?" Susan asked as they enjoyed coffee and dessert.

Kat stiffened next to him, and he could practically hear the walls coming up around her at the question. "No," Kat answered quietly, staring at the table in front of her. "I haven't talked to my family in eighteen years."

Sadness radiated from her in waves. Stuart could feel her bracing herself for more questions, or maybe having someone judge her for being estranged from her family. He hoped some day she would trust him enough to tell him the whole story about what happened to her.

As usual, his mother was able to make things better. Mom reached over to Kat and picked up her hand, giving it a firm squeeze.

"We're your family now Kat," she said, her voice serious. "You will always have a place here."

Kat visibly relaxed, then laughed as his father added, "God help you!"

They stayed another hour before Stuart got up to take Kat back to her apartment. Normally he would linger with his family for longer, but he sensed that despite her obviously having a good time, the evening had been a lot for his mate. The urge to protect her was strong, even if it was to keep her from feeling overwhelmed.

His mom sent them both off with warm hugs and leftover chili and cornbread for each of them to eat later.

"Your family is so...nice," Kat said softly as they pulled away from the house. "You guys are like a sitcom family or something."

"Yeah, they're pretty great," Stuart acknowledged. "And they really liked you."

"I really liked them too," she replied, her voice indicating her surprise. "I had a good time."

They spent the rest of short drive back to her apartment in a comfortable silence. Stuart had never been a big talker, and silence didn't bother him the way it did for some people. He was learning that his mate was the same. No extraneous chatter, no talking just to fill the silence.

This time the silence felt different. He could feel Kat's increased comfort around him. As annoyed as he had been with his mother for manipulating Kat into accept her dinner invitation, Stuart had to admit that it seemed to have softened Kat's opinion of him.

"Here you go," Stuart announced unnecessarily as he pulled into the parking lot behind the veterinary clinic. He stopped his truck near the stairs to her apartment, glancing over at his mate.

Kat took a deep breath, then turned to look at him, her eyes surprisingly vulnerable. "Would you, um, would you like to come up for a while?"

He watched her carefully even as his heart sped up so much he was sure it was going to pound its way out of his chest with excitement. Was she suggesting what he thought she was suggesting?

"Are you sure Kat? I don't want you to do anything you're not ready for."

She gave him a grateful smile, then placed her small hand on his arm. The skin tingled beneath her touch. "I can't promise you more than tonight Stuart, but I want you. I'm tired of denying it."

It wasn't a declaration of love, but it still meant the world to him. He gave her a wolfish smile.

"In that case Mate, I'm about to rock your world."

Kat

Kat rolled her eyes at his arrogant declaration. Although somehow she knew he was correct – she knew instinctively that her life would never be the same if she let Stuart come up, if she allowed their relationship to move to the next level.

She couldn't say what had changed. Maybe he had worn her down. Maybe the insistent whining of her tiger got to her. But something had definitely changed between them tonight, and she knew it was partly from having dinner with his family.

Seeing the obvious love and ease between the Greys was a revelation. They clearly liked each other, liked to spend time together. Everyone had pitched in for the meal and clean-up instead of the men barking orders while the women worked. Stuart and his dad had treated Susan and her mother – and Kat herself – with respect. As equals.

Seeing how a family could be different from hers had done more to melt the ice around her heart than anything else. During dinner she had found herself imagining that she was with them every week, talking and laughing and helping with dinner. She thought about being a part of this family, and suddenly it didn't feel so scary. Not scary at all.

Maybe she could trust Stuart. Maybe she owed it to herself to spend some time with him, to explore this relationship, and see what happened.

She was surprised to see her hands were shaking as she tried to unlock her front door. Part of her couldn't believe that she was inviting him into her private domain. She made it a rule to never have a guy in her place. It was too intimate, and she didn't want to have to worry about making them leave when she was done with them.

With Stuart her rules seemed to fall away, and everything almost felt like her first time all over again.

If he noticed her shaking hands he didn't say anything, but he laid his hand protectively on the small of her back which grounded her. She didn't want to analyze that too closely.

Stuart followed her into the apartment and looked around curiously, his shrewd eyes taking everything in. She had rented the apartment from Valerie furnished, but she had added her own touches. Pillows she had sewn out of fabric scraps. Several lush green plants. A few framed posters. It all made for an eclectic but homey space.

"Nice place," Stuart said. She glowed a little bit under his praise. "Now let's see the bedroom."

She laughed. "Feeling eager?" she teased, enjoying the comfortable banter between them.

"I'm afraid you'll change your mind," he confessed, his expression a tad bit vulnerable.

Her heart swelled with...affection. Not love, she told herself sternly. Just affection. Clearly she was warming up to the wolf. Her tiger made a disbelieving snort but otherwise was wisely silent.

Kat gave Stuart a smile and grabbed his large hand in hers. Her heart immediately sped up and her skin vibrated. She was instantly attuned to him and she wondered if it would be like this every time they touched each other.

She led him to the bedroom and swung him around by his hand, pushing him to sit on the bed. He dropped down with a small smirk, one eyebrow raised, content to let her take the lead.

She shrugged off her sweater, tossing it on the chair across the bed, and lifted the hem of her skirt up her thighs. She heard Stuart catch his breath as she lifted the fabric over her head and sent the dress flying to land on top of her discarded sweater.

Standing in front of him in only her underwear and cowboy boots she watched him watch her. His gaze was so intense she could feel it as if he were touching her.

"Beautiful," he growled. "You're fucking beautiful."

She leapt towards him with a growl. Unfortunately, he stood up and moved towards her at the exact same second. Their bodies collided midway and bounced off each other like a pinball hitting the side bumper. They fell in a heap on the floor, Kat on top.

"Well, that was just like a romantic movie," Kat laughed.

Stuart groaned. "Just the romantic start I was hoping for."

She moved her arm and felt the long hard length of his erection against her skin. The laughter immediately died in her throat as arousal hit her again like a tsunami. She crawled up his body until she was kneeling on either side of his waist, then leaned down and grabbed his hands. His eyes widened but he remained silent as she moved his hands to either side of his head, pinning them to the floor with her own hands.

"I've got you at my mercy now, wolf," she whispered with a satisfied smirk.

Without another word she lowered her head and kissed him. To her surprise, Stuart let her keep him trapped beneath her and let her set the pace. She pressed her lips against his for a long moment, then licked at the seam of his lips until he opened for her. She swept her tongue into his mouth as she settled her weight on his chest.

She explored his mouth thoroughly even while part of her wondered why things felt so different with Stuart compared to other guys. She had never felt this way from just a kiss. Well, honestly she had never felt this way ever, not with any other guy.

It's because he's our mate. Bite him.

Kat broke their kiss and lowered her head to press tiny kisses against the scruff on his jaw, then moved down to nip at his neck. For a second she wondered what it would be like to bite him, to give him the mate mark and be bound to him forever, but then she determinedly pushed that thought out of her mind.

Pushing herself to a sitting position, she released Stuart's hands and rolled off him.

"You're wearing too many clothes," she growled.

Stuart leapt up to standing with surprising speed, practically tearing his clothes off. Before Kat could get back on her own feet, he was naked. She took in his lightly furred chest, the ridges of his hard stomach, the well-defined muscles in his arms and legs. Stuart had the natural fitness of a shifter, honed by a career doing manual labor.

His thick cock jutting proudly out from his body, calling her attention. She stared at it and licked her lips. Stuart made a sound deep in his throat that was somewhere between a growl and a moan.

He stalked towards her. "Your turn."

Before she could process what was happening, Stuart released his claws and used the sharp edges to slice off her bra and panties. They fell to the ground in tatters, leaving her standing there just in her battered brown cowboy boots.

"Hey!" she protested. "I liked those! They were expensive!" She didn't add that she had only worn them for the first time tonight. For him.

"You were taking too long."

Stuart grabbed her by the waist and tossed her onto the bed as if she weighed nothing. She thrilled at his strength. She wasn't a small woman, and her body was dense with the muscles of her inner tiger as well as her generous curves. More than one guy had damn near thrown out his back attempting that same move.

He knelt on the bed and crawled over her like she had done to him. "My turn."

He lowered his mouth to kiss her, but she stopped him with a hand to the forehead.

"Wait!"

Stuart stilled immediately, his face taking on a look of concern. "What's the matter?"

She met his eyes. "We need rules."

He frowned but didn't respond. He hovered over her in push up position and waited for her to speak. She tried not to be impressed by the strength of his arms.

"First, and most importantly, you may not bite me."

Her tiger whined in protest, and she could swear that she heard his wolf do the same. The other night she had heard the story about Valerie and Colt and how he'd "accidentally" marked her in the heat of passion. No way was she falling for that trick.

"No breaking the skin. No claiming. No mating," she ticked off. "That is absolutely non-negotiable."

She saw a brief flash of hurt in his eyes, but he acquiesced. "I won't claim you, Mate," he promised. "I promise that I will wait until after you mark me first."

She started to argue that point, to tell him that she would never do that, but before she could speak he slowly lowered his body so that his pelvis pressed against hers. She groaned as she felt his delicious weight. He rolled his hips, bringing the tip of his cock just inside the lips of her pussy. She immediately felt a rush of moisture, her body crying out for him to move closer, and decided to move onto her other point.

"And my second rule," she continued. "I want you to promise you won't hang around after."

His brow wrinkled. "What do you mean?"

"No sleeping over. I don't do sleepovers."

"What if you want me to sleep over?"

"I won't."

"What if we are both so exhausted we both just pass out and I accidentally sleep over?"

"That's not going to happen," she said confidently.

"That sounds like a challenge to me."

"It's not." Yet she shivered with excitement. Would he rise to the challenge?

"What if I give you five orgasms?" he asked. "Can I sleep over then?"

She laughed incredulously. "Yeah sure, OK, if you give me five orgasms you can sleep over."

His eyes started glowing with his wolf and she felt compelled to add, "Just so you know, I have never been multi-orgasmic. Many people have tried, but I've never had more than one orgasm in a row, Stuart."

His smile was dark and full of promise. "Game on, Mate."

Stuart

Many people have tried, but I've never had more than one orgasm in a row.

His mate's words made his wolf puff up in challenge. He was both insanely jealous of every other man who dared to touch her, and thrilled at the idea that he would give her something she had never had. Not to brag, but he had never left a woman unsatisfied. And he certainly wasn't going to start with his mate.

He dropped the rest of his weight on her, trapping him between him and mattress, and kissed her deeply until they finally broke apart, gasping for air.

Start slid down until he was face level with her amazing breasts. They were plump and almost translucently pale. He squeezed them together between his hands, then lowered his mouth to take one dark pink nipple into his mouth. He licked around it, then added some suction, drawing on her. Her breath sped up.

He used his hands to roughly circle the other nipple, then pinched it firmly at the same time he bit down on the nipple in his mouth. His mate gasped and tried to shift beneath him, but she was trapped under his weight. He glanced up to see her eyes were closed tightly, her head moving from side to side.

He alternated between her breasts, switching between biting, sucking, and pinching, until Kat started making tiny noises in the back of her throat. She was already close to breaking apart, and he wondered if he could make her come just from stimulating her nipples.

Lowering his head again, he returned his attention to her breasts and began rolling his hips against the mattress between her legs. The movement caused his stomach to glide up and down across her mound, creating friction.

Kat's fingers tightened in his hair and once again he bit one nipple and pinched the other, harder this time. He repeated the pattern a few more times until she gave a keening wail and he felt her break apart beneath him.

"Oh!"

Only one word, but it said so much. Her body was shuddering and spasming violently as she rode out her orgasm. He didn't release her nipples until she softened with her release and sagged into the mattress.

He watched her until she opened her eyes and met his gaze. She looked dazed.

"That's one."

He gave her a feral smile, and her eyes widened.

Stuart slid down more, rubbing against her soft skin until his shoulders rested between the "V" of her legs. Spreading her even wider, he looked down at the glistening pink lips of her neatly trimmed pussy and growled deep in his throat.

"Mine!"

He slid his tongue into her weeping slit and licked her from bottom to top. She shuddered, and he repeated the action again and again, circling her clit roughly with each pass. She pushed against him half-heartedly a couple of times, but he continued to work her with his tongue. Kat wrapped her thighs around his head with enough force that he knew she was close again.

He redoubled his efforts and within a few minutes her back bowed off the bed and her body began to shudder. A soft moan escaped her lips, but she was otherwise quiet as her orgasm rolled through her body. Her wetness flooded his tongue and he lapped up her sweet cream as if he were the one who was a cat. He had never tasted anything so delicious.

"That's two."

She raised her head and looked at him smiling up at her from between her thighs.

"Fuck."

That one word was both a groan and a prayer. He felt pure masculine satisfaction that he was pleasing his mate so thoroughly. He wasn't going to stop until he had fucked all her reservations away, and made her forget every other man she'd been with.

"That's the idea," he told her, his voice deep and commanding. "I plan to ruin you for any other man."

He gripped her thighs and brought them up over his shoulders, changing the angle of her hips. He slid his hands under her ass and gripped her cheeks tightly, letting her feel the very tips of his claws on her skin. She swore softly again.

He speared his tongue into her opening and began sliding it in and out, doing with his tongue what he planned to do with his cock after he gave her another orgasm or two. It didn't take long until he felt her channel clench once again. This orgasm followed so close after the last one he would have thought it was just aftershocks if she wasn't coming so hard against his face that he could scarcely breathe.

When she finally came back down she pushed at his head. "Enough!" she gasped.

Stuart slid up to lay down next to her, wrapping one leg around her and resting his arm across her waist as she gradually got control of her breath. He leaned down and placed a gentle kiss on her lips.

"That's three."

Her eyes widened in shocked excitement as he added. "Now roll over Mate, I want you on your hands and knees for me."

For a second he thought she might argue, but she rolled away and did as he instructed. For all her independence, his mate seemed to like him to be dominant in the bedroom. He could work with that.

Stuart moved behind her on his knees, then lowered himself down to bracket her body. His poor aching cock slid between her ass cheeks and he heard her sharp intake of breath. He nipped her ear, then whispered, "Has anyone ever taken you there?"

She shuddered but stayed silent. He shifted and used one hand to land a sharp smack on her butt cheek.

"Hey!" she said indignantly, even while he could feel her heartbeat pick up with excitement. The more time he spent with her, the more he could tune into her emotions.

He smacked her cheek again. "Answer me."

She gave him a long-suffering sigh. "No. I've not been one for backdoor adventures."

He leaned back down and whispered in her ear. "You will be. But not tonight."

She shuddered again but didn't respond.

"Shall we work on number four?"

Before she could respond he shifted and pushed into her heat with one long hard stroke.

"Ah!" she wailed, her inner muscles impossibly tight around him despite already having three orgasms. He waited a few agonizing moments until she relaxed and adjusted to his girth, scattering gentle kisses over the top of her back.

Finally she gritted out, "Move Stuart!"

She didn't have to ask him twice. He pulled out and shoved back into her with such force she rocked forward. He wrapped one hand around her long silky hair and used it to pull her head back, controlling her. She moaned, apparently liking the bite of pain.

He started pounding into her roughly, hitting his pelvis against her ass with every stroke. She moaned again, loud and low, then made a purring sound deep in her chest. Her hips pushed back hard against him, meeting every stroke. Clearly his mate liked it a little rough.

He was dying to come, had been dying to come inside her since the moment he laid eyes on her and yet, he wanted to wait. He was going to get her to five orgasms or die trying. Stuart Grey had never backed down from a challenge and he certainly wasn't going to start now.

Releasing her hair, he pushed on her shoulders until she laid her face against the bedspread, pushing her ass up even more.

Thwack! He landed another sharp smack on her butt cheek and she gasped.

Thwack! He gave her other cheek the same attention.

"Do you like it when I spank you, Mate?" he growled.

When she didn't respond her gave her another sharp smack. "Answer me."

"Ah!!"

He gave her another spank.

"Yes. No. I don't know!"

He raised his hand again and she lifted her hips towards him as if welcoming the gentle pain. That was answer enough. He gave her a few more taps, alternating between cheeks. Her pale round globes pinked up quite nicely beneath his hand and he felt a sense of satisfaction as he marked her. He would never hurt her, but he was gratified that they both liked a little pain to enhance the pleasure. Stuart couldn't believe that the fates had sent him a mate who was so perfect for him.

Rising up on his knees, Stuart gripped her hips tightly and increased his pace, pounding into her so hard he could feel it in his bones. The room was filled with the sounds of their harsh breaths and the slapping of their flesh.

He didn't know how much longer he was going to last. His cock was harder than it had ever been before in his life. It was weeping with moisture as he mentally recited every boring statistic he could think of to stave off his orgasm. There was no way he was going to let himself come until he had secured the right to sleep over.

He couldn't say why this was such an important issue to him, but it really was. He wanted to break down her walls, wanted her to show her vulnerability, wanted her to let him get close to her. And most of all, he wanted nothing more than to wake up with her soft body in his arms.

"Get there!" he growled, reaching around to pinch her clit between his claws.

That was all it took. He felt her inner walls tighten around his cock like a vise. It was the best feeling ever. He could feel the waves of her orgasm even as she gasped beneath him, shuddering from the force of her orgasm. His mate was surprisingly quiet in bed.

He wanted one more thing before he came. He wanted her to come with his name on her lips. And he wanted that fifth orgasm.

"Time for number five," he announced.

He pulled out, then rolled her over onto her back. Lifting her legs onto his shoulders, he pushed back inside her but stayed still until she opened her eyes. Her pupils were huge, and she looked exhausted and relaxed and happy. He loved that he had put that look on her face. He loved that he had surprised her. He loved…her.

It hit him like a ton of bricks. He already knew she was his mate, the one person he wanted to spend the rest of his life with. But the mating urge was more about his wolf side. His human side, the logical side, hadn't really analyzed his feelings until just now. Man and wolf were in complete agreement: Kat was the only woman they wanted for the rest of their lives.

He slid out until only the tip of his cock was inside her, the slid slowly back in. She closed her eyes and he immediately stopped. "Look at me!" he growled.

She opened her eyes and he caught her gaze, communicating everything with his eyes that he longed to say with his lips. Knowing instinctively that she wasn't ready to talk about their feelings for each other, even though it was clear to both of them. The mate bond was already activating between them, even though they hadn't marked each other yet, and he knew she was sensing his emotions the same way he was feeling hers. He could see it in her eyes clear as day.

He gave her several long, slow strokes, while holding eye contact. Somehow that was more intimate than anything they had done tonight.

He picked up the pace slightly. "Say my name," he growled, his wolf so close to the surface it was all he could do to keep the animal from bursting through his skin and sinking its teeth into the neck of their mate.

Her eyes widened in confusion. "What?"

"I want you to say my name, Mate. I want to hear you call out for me as I make you come on my cock. I want to know that you feel this as much as I feel it."

He kept up his slow but steady pace. With her legs over his shoulders, he was grinding hard against her mound with every pass, stimulating her already sensitive clit.

His heart was pounding so hard he thought he might pass out. The base of his spine was tingling, a sure sign of his impending orgasm.

He lowered his head and took her mouth in a kiss that was a sweet as it was savage. He pushed his tongue in and out, matching the pace of their hips.

Her muscles were tightening around him again and he felt the adrenaline of being so close to his goal. His hips sped up until he was once again pounding into her roughly, setting a punishing pace. Her fingers wrapped around his shoulders, unable to do more than hold on, and he felt her draw blood as her claws extended and broke through the skin.

He lowered one hand to her throat, pressing just hard enough for her to feel his control over her. Her eyes widened, but he only saw excitement, not fear.

"Say it."

He snapped his hips back and slid back into her so hard he felt the tip of his cock hit her cervix. She moaned loudly.

"Say. My. Name."

He gave her one, two, three more hard strokes and she shattered beneath him.

"Stuart!"

His name escaped her lips on a long wail and still maintaining eye contact with her, he finally let go.

"Kat! Mate!"

Jet after jet of his seed pulsed out of him, painting the inside of her womb, marking her with his scent. It wasn't a mate bite, but he knew that any other shifter would smell him on her, would know that they had been together. At least for the next day or two.

He thrust into her again and again as he continued to come, his eyesight going fuzzy and his head light. It was the longest and most intense orgasm of his life and he felt quite sure that if he died at this moment, it would all be worth it.

When it was finally over he collapsed on top of her, panting for a few long minutes, before he rolled over and pulled her into the crook of his arm. Kat snuggled up against him and laid her head on his chest, wrapping her arm around his waist and sliding one leg on top of his. His heart swelled with happiness as she willingly snuggled up against him.

"What was that about never having multiple orgasms?" he asked her, hearing the masculine pride in his own voice.

"You win," she whispered sleepily. "You can sleep over."

As she drifted to sleep on top of him he knew his life would never be the same. And that was awesome.

Kat

The next three weeks flew by. She and Stuart had spent every night together since that first time, alternating between their two houses. Kat tried not to spend too much time analyzing how easily she fell into a relationship pattern with him. For now, it felt comfortable and exciting.

They got together every night when they were both done with work, they had dinner together, and slept curled up together, as close as possible. They had made love every single night, usually more than once and some days, like today, in the morning too.

Kat smiled and stretched as she remembered Stuart waking her up early this morning with his fingers between her legs as he spooned her. When she was panting for him he slid her leg up and entered her from behind, slowly bringing them both to a soul shattering orgasm before they fell back asleep again.

She had always had a healthy sex drive, and none of the full humans that she had dated over the years could keep up with her. But Stuart, he could keep going until she collapsed into the mattress with exhaustion, begging him to stop. She loved it. He didn't treat her like some piece of glass that would shatter. Instead, he gave her the rough, raw sex that she craved. That they both did. She loved nothing more than to see Stuart lose control and know that she had been the cause.

It was Sunday, and for the fourth week in a row she was going with Stuart to his family's Sunday dinner. She never would have thought that it was possible, but she loved hanging out with Stuart's family. They had immediately welcomed her into the fold, treating her like one of their own. Gail already felt more like a mother than her own mother ever had.

She only hoped they wouldn't hate her when she and Stuart broke up. Because eventually, this thing had to burn itself out, right? Happily ever after was only for fairy tales.

He's our mate, he will never tire of us.

Meanwhile everyone in town was wondering why they didn't seal the deal. Everywhere she went, people made comments about her and Stuart making it official and becoming mates. It was weird how invested everyone in town seemed to be in their relationship.

She knew Stuart was all in. More than once in the heat of passion she had to remind him not to mark her as she felt the scratch of his fangs on her neck.

It wasn't just Stuart though. Her tiger had been increasingly difficult to deal with lately. Although she was happy to be near her m...., near Stuart, the tiger was impatient for them to mark him. To make it official. No amount of human reasoning could discourage her.

Several times Kat had felt her own fangs start to descend during sex, the urge to bite Stuart almost overwhelming, before she was able to wrangle her tiger back into submission. Sometimes she wondered why she continued to resist what seemed almost inevitable, then she would remember her mother and the women in her birth streak, and her resolve would strengthen again.

He was being patient – for now – but Kat didn't know how long she could put him off. And if she refused to commit, would she lose him? Her tiger whined low and long in her head at the very idea. Honestly, the human in her wasn't happy about it either. And that's what really scared her. She was growing much too attached to him.

Since they both had some work to catch up on this weekend they had each spent most of the day at their respective jobs, and planned to just meet up at his parents' house for the family dinner. Kat got there late because she had gotten absorbed in her work and lost track of time. It was a new thing for her to have people expecting to see her at a certain time.

She rushed over to Stuart's parents' house and his dad let her in with a smile.

"Come on back, dear," he said, offering her a warm hug. "Everyone is in the kitchen."

She took in the domestic scene in front of her with a smile. Stuart was pulling a roast out of the oven while Susan made a salad. Their mother was icing a cake for dessert but came over to give Kat a big hug.

She sniffed audibly, then reached up to move the collar of Kat's shirt to one side and then the other.

"Still no mate bite?" she asked, looking at Kat curiously. "What are you two waiting for?"

Kat had a feeling Stuart's mom knew very well that Kat was the one who was hesitant. Maybe she was imagining it, but she felt like there was a bit of judgement in his mom's eyes. She realized everyone was staring at her, and she felt a tinge of a blush color her cheeks.

"Ma, please." Stuart's voice had a warning. "Don't start."

Gail walked over and gave him a smack on the back of the head. "Hey!" he growled indignantly.

"Don't you 'hey' me young man," she grumbled. "I'm not getting any younger you know. I want both of my kids settled down and giving me some grandpups."

"Oh no, don't bring me into this," Susan called.

"We'll get there Ma," Stuart said, shooting his mother a quelling look. "Let it go."

"Let it go?" she asked incredulously. "How long are you and your mate going to mess around before you make a commitment? You met several weeks ago already. You don't need to date forever like the full humans do, not when you already know you are meant to be together. And clearly you're not having any issues in the bedroom, I can smell you on each other every time you're here."

Mr. Grey stayed silent, keeping out of the fray, but watched everything carefully.

Kat felt a stab of panic. Grandpups? Commitment? This felt like it was getting way too serious way too fast for her. This is what she got for relaxing her guard. Things with Stuart felt too easy and yet, way too complicated. But now there were so many expectations. His family was judging her, and everyone would be mad at her when they broke up.

She had come to love Stuart's family and it suddenly hit her that she would lose them as well when it came time to say goodbye to Stuart. And the longer she spent with them, the more she got attached, the worse it would be to say goodbye.

If she was honest with herself, it wasn't only his family that she was growing to depend on. She suddenly realized that Stuart had wormed his way into her life so effectively that every day it became harder to imagine breaking up with him. And yet she knew she had to. It was the only way to protect herself.

She felt her chest tighten in panic. Her breath was coming in short gasps. What had happened to all the oxygen in here? She couldn't breathe. Oh my god, is this what an anxiety attack felt like?

"I'm sorry. I can't do this anymore. I have to go," she choked out.

"Kat..." Stuart moved towards her and she held up a hand to stop him.

"No Stuart, you have dinner with your family," she gasped. "I really need to go. I just...I can't do this!"

"Please don't go Kat, I'm sorry I pushed you," Gail offered. "I didn't mean any harm. Truly."

Kat shook her head. Her brain was buzzing so loud she scarcely heard herself repeat, "I have to go. I have to go." She could feel herself start to lose it as she became more and more panicked.

She turned on her heel and raced out of the house, heading towards the street. She knew Stuart would follow her, even as she hoped that he wouldn't. He caught up with her at the end of the driveway, his hand on her arm pulling her to a stop.

"Kat. Please wait."

She rounded on him, suddenly furious with him.

"You see? This is exactly why I told you to leave me alone in the beginning." Her voice rose angrily. "I thought we could just have some fun and date for a while and that was totally stupid of me."

"Kat..."

"No. I didn't ask for any of this Stuart. I don't want people have expectations of me like this. I don't want to just be someone's mate. I don't want to just be the little wife, cleaning your house and popping out cubs until I have no identity of my own anymore."

"That's not what's going to happen," he said softly, stroking her arm with his warm hand. The motion was comforting, which just made her angrier. At him, at herself, at the world.

It was tempting to lean into him, take comfort from him. But she couldn't rely on him. She couldn't give up her independence. She had almost died to be free.

He seemed to respect her independence right now, but she couldn't risk getting mated and him changing the rules. She had seen firsthand how males could be charming in their pursuit, but things would change once they finally got what they wanted.

She looked up and met his gaze head on, wanting him to see the truth in her eyes. Her breath still came in short, panicked gasps.

"You're a great guy Stuart and I've, um, I've had fun," she said. "But this isn't going to work."

"Kat..."

"No, let me finish." She took a step back, so his hand dropped from her arm. She knew she could think more clearly without the distraction of his touch. "I need you to hear me clearly. I told you the first day we met that I didn't want a mate. That I didn't want you. Nothing has changed."

She ignored the flash of hurt on his face.

"Nothing?" he asked softly. There was so much pain in that one word she nearly bowed under it, but instead she took a deep breath and straightened her spine.

"I like you a lot, but this is getting way too serious for me. I'm too damaged for someone like you," she told him. "I don't want to hurt you, and if we keep doing what we're doing that's exactly what's going to happen."

She gave him a sad smile. "I'm not the mate for you Stuart. But I hope you find someone who is. Find yourself a nice wolf who can give your mom the grandpups she's waiting for."

She felt a stab of pain at her own words, her tiger snarling and biting inside her at the thought of her mate being with anyone else.

"Please let me go."

Stuart stood on the driveway, looking like a man who had lost his best friend. She felt his pain, but she knew that she had to be strong. She had to keep them from getting in too deep and hurting each other more than they already had.

"Goodbye," she whispered.

This time when she ran off, he didn't follow.

She ran all the way home, gasping for breath the whole way, until she reached the sanctuary of her apartment. She had never given Stuart a key, but she locked herself in her bathroom just in case. She knew she wouldn't be strong enough to resist him if she let him close to her again.

As she slid down the wall to collapse on the cold tile Kat did something she hadn't done since she left home eighteen years ago. She cried herself to sleep.

Stuart

"Honey, I'm so sorry!"

His mom must have been watching from the window because she pounced on him as soon he walked in the door.

"I was only teasing you two."

He gave her a skeptical look but didn't answer. The pain was making it hard for him to breathe.

"OK, well I was trying to give her a little nudge I admit, but I didn't think she would have such a strong reaction," his mother continued. "I'm sorry for meddling like that."

"She broke up with me," Stuart told her, feeling like he wanted to cry for the first time since he broke his arm when he was nine years old. Deep inside him, his wolf howled in sorrow at the loss of its mate.

"Come sit down."

His mother led him to the table where the rest of the family had already sat down. He dropped into a chair and stared blankly at the plate of food his mom put in front of him. What was he going to do? He couldn't lose her. She was everything to him. Already he felt her lose as a sharp pain in his chest.

"What are you going to do son?" his dad asked. "You know I don't normally butt into your private life...," he stopped to give his wife a reproving look, "but you've already met your mate and started bonding. Even without completing the mating process, you're still tied together. People have literally gone crazy after being separated from their fated mate."

He shook his head miserably. "I don't know. I was trying to give her some time to get used to the idea, but now she's totally shut me out again."

"What did she say exactly?" Dad asked.

"She said she never should have gotten close to me." He shook his head. "She told me to go find a wolf who wants a mate and babies. That she didn't want to lose her identity and independence."

"She's gotten to know you already, so what's the problem?" Mom asked. "She knows you're not the kind of man who would subjugate a woman."

"The problem is she has gotten to know him...," his sister started.

Dad frowned and interrupted, "Don't kick a wolf when he's down Susan."

She huffed. "No Dad, that's my point. Logically she knows if she pushes Stuart away he will respect her wishes. He won't be one of those alphahole shifter dudes that will go throw her over his shoulder and bite her whether she likes it or not."

Stuart looked up. "Throw her over my shoulder?" That idea had some appeal. His wolf chuffed in agreement.

Susan shook her head. "No, because that's exactly what she thinks you're going to do."

"Huh?" Stuart was confused. "You just said she doesn't think I'm like that, and that I'll respect her wishes."

"I think deep down she hopes that if you get mad enough you will lose your easy-going ways. That if she pushes you enough, you will let your wolf take over," Susan explained. "She knows if it was up to your wolf he would take the decision away from her and just mark her. She also knows that's what her tiger wants to happen. So she's pushing you to lose your temper."

"But why?"

"Then she's not responsible if things go badly and she ends up unhappy with you later," Susan continued. "It's one thing if she voluntarily gives up her independence. It's another if she's forced into it because you lose control. She can blame you for taking that choice away. She can tell herself that you're just like all the guys she grew up with. You'll prove her fears were correct, even if you taking that decision away from her is what she secretly hopes for."

"I would never force her to do anything," he said stubbornly. "I love her too much to force her into something that she says she doesn't want. Even though I know that you're right and on some level, she wants this as much as I do."

"That's why you need to force her to be the one who makes the decision to mate, big brother. Make her choose you."

"What are you suggesting Susan?"

"She told you to find a nice young wolf to mate right? You need to do just that."

Kat

It had been almost a week since she had seen Stuart. Almost a week since she had broken his heart, along with her own. Almost a week since she had woken up cold and alone on her bathroom floor, eyes swollen nearly shut from crying, and realized that she was in love with her mate but ruined their chance to be together. Almost a week of her tiger ripping up her insides, whining for her to go to Stuart and make it all right.

Despite her telling Stuart to leave her alone, Kat had fully expected him to follow her and try to change her mind. She had argued with herself incessantly about whether she would acquiesce and agree to mate with him when he tried to win her back.

But he hadn't tried to win her back. To her dismay, the past six days it had been totally radio silence. He hadn't texted, hadn't stopped by, hadn't sent gifts like he had done in the beginning. She told herself that she was glad he had finally accepted her wishes, but deep down, she was shocked and disappointed and heart stick that he had given up so easily. Maybe he didn't care as much as she thought.

All week she had gone through the motions. She got up, got dressed, and went to work instead of staying in her bed feeling sorry for herself.

One thing she hadn't expected was that everyone in town would know about their break-up five minutes after it happened. She smiled and brushed aside people's concern or well-meaning advice about the break-up. She ignored the curious stares of people wondering what was wrong with her that she would reject such a great mate like Stuart.

People in Greysden hadn't hesitated to give Kat their opinion on what she was missing out on. She had run into Mr. and Mrs. Xenakis on the street, and they seemed more upset about the break-up than she was. Well, maybe not quite...

The truth was, she missed him terribly. She couldn't eat. She couldn't sleep without Stuart laying in bed next to her, which was crazy considering that she had slept alone all those years. Her chest ached with loss every moment of the day.

She told herself that the pain would go away eventually, but she was still wallowing in a misery of her own making. And she hated herself even more for hurting Stuart. The look of devastation on his face when she broke up with him would haunt her for the rest of her life.

She told herself that in the end they would both realize that she was right, and she was better off alone. Just like she had always been. She reminded herself that Stuart would be better off with a mate who could be what he wanted her to be. But it was getting harder and harder to believe that they were better off apart the longer she was away from Stuart.

We shouldn't be apart, her tiger spat angrily. *We will be in pain until we are with our mate.*

About a million times a day she wondered if she should reach out to Stuart, convince him to give her another chance. Then she talked herself out of it again. It's not like he was pursuing her anymore. Clearly he had given up on her, and she couldn't blame him after the way she had treated him.

She heard a knock on the door of her workroom and looked up to see her boss Gina standing in the doorway. As usual Gina was smiling cheerfully and dressed to the nines in an outfit she had designed herself.

"Hey Kat, how are you doing?" she asked, doing that head tilt that everyone seemed to do around her, as if she was five seconds from breaking down. Which was probably accurate. She had cried more in the last few days than she had in her entire life put together. Her pain was like a heavy cloak, weighing her down.

"I'm totally fine Gina, really," she lied, plastering on a fake smile.

"Oh good, since you're fine you are coming out with us tonight for our monthly girls' night at Murphy's Bar. I meant to mention it the other day."

Kat's mind immediately flashed to the last happy hour she went to with Gina, the one where Stuart showed up and walked her home. How it had been the beginning of him worming his way into her affections...She shook her head.

"Thanks for the invite but I'm not really up to a happy hour tonight, and..."

"Nonsense," Gina interrupted her. "If you're really fine with the break-up, there's no reason to avoid having fun with your friends. Besides, maybe we'll both meet someone new tonight."

Gina waggled her eyebrows suggestively, making Kat's tiger sit up angrily. There was no way her tiger would consider dating anyone else so soon.

Not ever, the tiger snarled.

"I don't..."

"Nope," Gina interrupted again, her face taking on a stubborn look. "Enough wallowing young lady. We've both worked hard all week and deserve some fun. Now get your purse so we can leave. I will not take 'no' for an answer."

An hour later she sat at the same table as her last visit to the bar. Only Gina and Valerie were there this time, to Kat's relief. She didn't think she was ready to face Stuart's sister after everything that had happened between them. It was too bad really, because she and Susan had really clicked and could have been good friends if Kat hadn't smashed her brother's heart into a million pieces.

Kat picked at a salad, only half listening to the conversation around her. Suddenly a piece of bread flew through the air and hit her in the forehead. She looked up to see Gina glaring at her. "What?"

"For someone who keeps insisting that she's totally OK with her break-up, you seem pretty mopey," Gina said. "Are you sure you don't want to talk about it?"

Kat shook her head. "There's nothing to talk about. We wanted different things and it didn't work out. Now we both need to move on."

"Speaking of moving on..." Valerie shot her a look she couldn't decipher.

"What?"

Valerie nodded at something behind Kat's head. "It's just that Stuart seems to have moved on. Pretty damn quickly too."

She spun around in her seat to see what Valerie was talking about. What the hell? Stuart sat at a tiny table in the corner, talking to a beautiful woman in a very short black skirt and low-cut red blouse. She looked super young and...perky.

What happened to that guy who said he loved her? The guy who said he wanted to spend the rest of his life as her mate? Was it all a lie?

Kat watched in horror as the woman leaned forward and put her hand on Stuart's arm, a flirty smile on her face. He smiled back and placed his other hand on top of hers. Then he leaned forward, moving in like he was going to kiss the girl.

And that's when Kat lost it. And so did her tiger.

Get that woman away from our mate! the tiger screeched, pressing against her and urging her to shift so she could kill the competition. Kat leapt up so quickly she knocked her chair over, letting out a growl of rage.

"What are you doing?" Gina called as she moved away.

Kat ignored her and stalked over to Stuart's table, glaring at the couple the whole way. She sniffed and identified the girl as a wolf. *Figures he would hook up with a pretty little wolf, she thought bitterly,* completely overlooking the fact that she had told Stuart to do exactly that.

When she reached the table, Kat slammed her hands down between Stuart and the girl, making their freshly delivered beers spill over the rim of their glasses. Heads turned in their direction, and conversation in the bar ground to a halt.

Stuart looked up with forced casualness. "Oh hey Kat, how's it going?"

He greeted her like she was a casual acquaintance, not the woman he had laid next to in bed and shared all his hopes and dreams.

"This is your ex?" the girl asked before Kat could respond. Her voice was high and breathy. "You never told me she was so old." She leaned forward more, offering Stuart a better view of her generous cleavage, and shooting Kat a triumphant look.

Kat's vision tinged with a red haze as adrenaline-fueled rage swept through her body. She had never been this mad in her entire life. She was shaking with the force of it, and so was her tiger.

"Stuart?" she ground out from between clenched teeth. "May I have a word with you outside?"

Stuart shook his head, keeping his gaze fixed on the girl. "Can we catch up later Kat? I'm having a drink with my...friend here."

Kat wrapped her hand around his wrist, roughly drawing it away from the girl's hand, and yanked Stuart up to standing. She was dimly aware that every eye in the place was watching the drama unfold.

"Now Stuart!"

She turned and dragged him by the wrist towards the back of the bar as he called, "I'll be right back, baby."

"OK honey," the girl giggled behind them.

Kat growled angrily. The crowd parted in front of them as she stalked through the bar. She pulled Stuart out the back door and into the alley behind the bar, then shoved him against the brick wall with a hard thump. Adrenaline and anger made her even stronger than usual.

"What the hell is wrong with you?" Stuart snapped.

"I can't believe you're here with that, that, that little wolf!" she snapped, glaring at him as if she could strike him down with just her eyes. "She's young enough to be your daughter for god's sake."

Stuart straightened to his full height and glared back at her. "She's only fifteen years younger than me. Not that it's any of your business Kat. You broke up with me, remember?"

"Yeah, I broke up with you FIVE days ago and you're already dating?" Kat snarled. "What happened to all the 'you're my mate we're soul mates' talk? Was that all a lie?"

He gave her an arrogant smirk. "You were very clear you didn't want to be mates," he reminded her. "You told me to move on and I took your advice. Found myself a nice wolf who wants to be a mate to someone and wants to be a mother."

"You're actually going to mate that little girl?" she said incredulously.

"Why not?" he answered, his voice annoyingly calm. "She's beautiful and my family just adores her. We have a great time together."

Before she could even process what she was doing, Kat leapt forward towards him, eliminating the space between them. She grabbed his shirt and ripped it open, sending buttons flying all over the alley. In the space of a breath her fangs descended, and she lowered her mouth to his shoulder, sinking her teeth deep into his flesh with a growl.

His blood flowed into her mouth, faintly tinged with copper, as she marked him in the spot that would tell every shifter he encountered that he belonged to her, and no one else. She felt a zap of energy as they became connected through the mate bond.

"Try mating her now," she spat as she pulled away from him.

He looked at her in amazement, his fingers going to his neck. "I can't believe you marked me."

Suddenly the magnitude of what she had done hit her. Kat stepped back, her rage receding as she stared at the wound on his neck. What had she done? She tried to find it in her to be upset, but somehow she couldn't regret following her instincts for once.

Meanwhile her tiger was running around in joyful circles in her mind. *You finally marked our mate!*

"I...I...um, I guess I did."

Stuart stalked towards her and this time it was her back that hit the brick wall. He placed one hand on either side of her head, leaning down to stare into her eyes. She couldn't help but meet his intense gaze.

"Why? I thought you didn't want to have a mate." His scent was an odd mixture of confusion and triumph.

"Maybe I changed my mind," she whispered, suddenly feeling foolish. Marking people without permission was frowned upon in the shifter community. What if he had changed his mind? What if he didn't want to be her mate anymore? What if he was really interested in that kid?

"Why?" he asked.

She stared at him silently until he prompted again, "Why did you mark me Kat?"

"I couldn't stand seeing you with that girl," she finally admitted with a burst of annoyance. "I couldn't stand by and let you mate her."

"Why?"

The air was thick as energy pulsed between them. Despite her agitation, Kat was aware of how close Stuart was, the heat of his body warming up the coldness that had sunk into her body since they broke up. She wanted nothing more than to curl up against him right now, but first she needed to tell him the truth.

"Because I love you OK?" she huffed, pushing out from between his arms and pacing away a few steps before walking back again.

"You love me?" he asked.

"Yes, damn it, I do!" she responded. "I saw you with her and I thought about you moving on, spending your life with someone else, and even though it's what I thought I wanted, when I saw it happening it made me crazy and jealous. I knew I had to mark you and make you mine. Are you happy now?"

He grabbed her hand and pulled her to his chest, wrapping his hands around her waist. Instinctively she moved closer. His smile was as wide as she'd ever seen it. Something inside her settled and she suddenly felt calm.

"Yes, as a matter of fact, I am happy now," he said, leaning down to nip her ear. "Oh, and by the way, that girl is my cousin."

"What?"

"The girl I was with is my cousin Stacy," he told her with a smile.

"You tricked me?" she said incredulously.

"Susan said that the only way you would realize that we were meant to be together was if you thought I was falling for someone else," he explained. "I guess she was right."

"So, what happens now?" she asked, suddenly feeling more vulnerable than she had in her entire life.

He dropped a kiss on her forehead, then grabbed her hand.

"Now we go home," he answered as he started pulling her down the alley. "And when we get there, I'm going to mate the hell out of you."

And he did.

Epilogue – Stuart

3 years later...

"I hate you! I hate you and I'm sorry I ever bit you in that damn alley!"

Stuart grabbed his mate's hand and she squeezed hard enough to draw blood, even with her human fingers. "Kat, honey..."

"Don't 'Kat honey' me, you...you...dog! This is all your fault."

The squeezing intensified as another contraction hit. His mate grimaced in pain as the doctor encouraged her to push. He could see the effort it took. His mate was so strong, and she looked beautiful swollen with his child. He had never loved her more.

"One more push momma, come on, you can do it."

Kat glared at the doctor. She opened up her mouth, no doubt to cuss out the doctor, but Stuart cut her off with a kiss. She reciprocated by biting his lip – hard.

"Get off me!" she screeched, pushing against his chest. "This is how we got in this situation in the first damn place!"

Stuart wisely stayed quiet as she bore down and gave a final push. But he kept a hold of her hand the entire time, offering her strength and comfort until they finally heard the squealing cry of their child.

"Congratulations, it's a girl!" the doctor said.

A few minutes later, the doctor laid a sticky, screaming baby on Kat's chest. Her arms wrapped around the baby automatically. The baby's face was red and irritated and in that moment, she looked so much like his mate that Stuart had to bite his lip to keep from laughing. His heart swelled with love, and he leaned down and kissed the baby's soft forehead.

"Happy birthday, little girl."

"She's beautiful," Kat whispered tiredly.

He ran his hand over Kat's sweaty hair and kissed her cheek. "So are you. Nice job with that delivery, Mate."

Kat gave him a beautiful smile. "I'm sorry I yelled at you."

He laughed. "I remembered that part from last time."

As if summoned, the door to the hospital room opened and their two-year-old son Daniel toddled in, closely followed by Stuart's parents. His mom rushed over to check on Kat. The two had been thick as thieves ever since he and Kat had been mated.

Stuart picked up Daniel, settling him on his hip, and said, "Look Daniel, you have a sister."

Daniel scrunched his nose. "She's ugly."

The baby screeched in response, causing Daniel to cry too. The room filled with crying.

Kat fell back against the pillows, clearly exhausted. "Yeah this having siblings thing is going to go great Stuart, I hope you're happy."

He leaned down and kissed her gently. "I sure am, Mate. I sure am."

***

Did you like this book? Show the love and leave me a review. Reviews are like puppies, they make you feel happy.

Be sure to keep reading for a special except from "Until You Came Along", available now from select retailers.

Special Preview

Until You Came Along by Rose Bak

Jen heard the rumbling from all the way in the kitchen. Wiping her hands on a towel, she walked to the front porch to watch the two large buses drive up the long driveway to the farmhouse. Belching smoke, they idled and came to a stop, one behind the other.

Although it wasn't even 10 a.m. yet, the sun shone brightly in the summer sky, showcasing the dust left in the wake of the parked buses. A bird squawked loudly in the sudden silence as a serious looking young woman scurried out of the first bus, glasses askew, a clipboard gripped in one hand, cellphone in another. Two large mountains of men followed her, hulking shadows.

"Jen Oliver? The band is here. We'll just come in and...." she moved to enter the house, but Jen stood her ground, blocking the door.

"Where are they?" she asked the woman, her tone icy. "And who are you exactly?"

The woman looked flustered for a brief moment before her stern mask fell back down again. She shuffled her cell phone into the hand with the clipboard and stuck out her now-free hand to shake. "I'm Simone. I manage the band."

Jen ignored her hand. "Well, manage them out of those buses. They don't get to send the help out to greet their sister."

Simone looked confused as she dropped her hand back to her side. "They're all sleeping. They had a late night. We'll just come in and check...."

"Still up all night and sleeping all day, huh? That's been the same since they were teenagers." Jen shook her head. On the farm they had all been taught the value of hard work – up before dawn, work all day, and early to bed. Somehow those lessons hadn't really stuck with her brothers despite her grandparents' best efforts over the years.

Of course, the boys, as she still thought of them, had been away from the farm for ten years now, chasing fame and fortune as the biggest boy band to hit the charts since N Sync. Like the band that came before them, the Oliver Boys had grown up but continued to enchant teenage girls across the world with their pop tunes.

Simone clearly felt protective of the boys. "They played last night in Wichita you know," she said sternly. "The show went until almost midnight, then they met the fans and press for hours after."

"By meet the fans and press do you mean got drunk and partied?" Jen's tone did little to hide her opinion of the boys and their reputation for debauched partying.

Simone shook her head. "They've mostly settled down now. There's not as much partying as there used to be when they were younger. But they still need to make an effort to meet people, it's part of the job. Now we'll just come in and...."

Jen shook her head. "Well," she drawled. "When they wake up from their so-called job, you send them on in. The rest of you need to find some other place to bunk. I'm not running a hotel for drunken roadies here."

A slight movement behind Simone caught Jen's eyes. One of the giant men flanking Simone shook with repressed laughter, his mouth twisted in a smirk but his face otherwise impassive. Jen looked at him for the first time. He was the size of a small tank, several inches over 6 feet tall, with impossibly wide shoulders and large biceps. His hair was a dark blond, "dishwater blonde" her grandma would call it, worn military short. He was dressed all in black, and she noticed a gun on the shoulder holster. Jen wondered why he felt he needed a gun out here in the middle of nowhere. She felt him watching her and she raised her eyes to his, a shiver of awareness coursing through her, although she couldn't make out his eyes behind the dark sunglasses.

"Miss Oliver..." Simone started again.

"Jen"

"OK, then, Jen, we need to do a security sweep before the boys come in. If you could just move aside, we'll get started." Simone nodded decisively.

"A security—-what the hell are you talking about?"

Simone turned to the man who'd been staring at Jen earlier. "This is Nick, he's head of security for the band. He'll be doing a security sweep and assessment with Brian here," she pointed at the second silent man.

"We don't need a security sweep. This place is as safe as it comes. We don't even lock the doors in these parts."

Simone shook her head again, vibrating with irritation and clearly not used to people disobeying her orders. "No way. The boys don't go anywhere without a security check ahead of time. I'm afraid I have to insist."

Jen shot her a look filled with venom, her tone as cold as ice. "You can insist all you like but this is my property. You have no right to it, and neither do the boys. Y'all can just run along now, I'm not having some ginormous strangers poking around my property. Don't make me sic the dogs on you." Simone's mouth dropped open.

This was an empty threat. Jen's three dogs looked mean, but they were incurably friendly. They were just as likely to lick a person to death as bite them. Jen had a sneaking suspicion that if someone tried to kill her the dogs would jump over her body and leave with the killer. But these music people didn't need to know that. If there was one thing Jen hated, it was music people. They were way too self-important and proud.

"Excuse me ma'am," the guy called Nick interrupted.

"Jen," she repeated, a trace of irritation in her tone.

He inclined his head. "Sorry. Jen. As Simone mentioned, I'm head of security for the band. We've had some issues and I would be very appreciative if my team could just poke around for a bit and make sure there's nothing amiss." His tone was deferential and charming, which only heightened Jen's suspicions.

"What kind of issues?"

"I'm afraid I'm not at liberty to discuss that ma—I mean Jen."

"Then I'm afraid I'm not at liberty to grant you access to my property. You step foot off that driveway, and I'll shoot you myself, right after I set the dogs on you. And you," she pointed at Simone, "better make sure no one bothers me again until I see those boys on my porch." She spun on her heel and slammed the door. It was going to be a long day.

***

For more of Jen's story, check out Until You Came Along by Rose Bak. Available at select online retailers.

About the Author

Rose Bak has been obsessed with reading since she got her first library card at age five. A passionate reader and a frequent blogger, she writes both fiction and nonfiction. Rose lives in the Pacific Northwest with her family and special needs dogs.

Please sign up for my newsletter[1] to get a free book and keep up to date on all the Rose Bak romance news.

1. https://storyoriginapp.com/giveaways/62ee758e-068f-11eb-904e-c373f6014fe1

Other Books by Rose Bak

The Diamond Bay Contemporary Romance Series

Brand New Penny

Fresh as a Daisy

Right as Rain

Bite-Sized Shifters Series

Wolf Doctor

Kat's Dog

The Good with Numbers Holiday Novella Contemporary Romance Series

Love Unmasked

The Thanksgiving Scrooge

Maid for Christmas

Countdown to Love

Valentine's Lottery

The Oliver Boys Band Contemporary Romance Series

Until You Came Along

Rock Star Teacher

Rock Star Writer

Rock Star Neighbor

Loving the Holidays Series

Dating Santa

New Year's Steve

Beach Wedding

Together Again

Non-fiction

What to Do If You Find a Cougar in Your Living Room: Self-Care in an Uncaring World

Catch up with these and other stories. Join my newsletter for more information[1] or follow my author page on your favorite retailer.

---

1. *https://storyoriginapp.com/giveaways/62ee758e-068f-11eb-904e-c373f6014fe1*

Don't miss out!

Visit the website below and you can sign up to receive emails whenever Rose Bak publishes a new book. There's no charge and no obligation.

https://books2read.com/r/B-A-VATM-JBHPB

BOOKS 2 READ

Connecting independent readers to independent writers.